OPENING PANDORA'S BOX
BOOK 2
OLLIE WATCHES HIS WIFE WITH ANOTHER MAN

PETE ANDREWS

This is a work of fiction. ***All characters are of legal age and are 18 years old or older.***

First Edition. October 2023.

ABOUT THE AUTHOR

I write sexy romances. I used to publish under *xleglover* and *Flash of Stocking* on various sites.

My stories are romances, so they explore the feelings, emotions and relationships of the characters. My stories have an emotional edge to them. The characters have thrilling adventures, but there's pain there too, at least for some of them.

I try to write stories that seem like real life. Yes, the situations are extreme, but I hope you come away thinking, *"Yes, I can see how that might happened."*

You can find my books at *Amazon Kindle* and *Smashwords*. Also, *Barnes & Noble, Apple Books,* and *Rakuten kobo*. If you'd like to join my mailing list or would like to send me a question or feedback, please email me at *peteandrews1701@gmail.com*.

BOOKS BY PETE ANDREWS

Faithful Wife's Fall From Grace (on-going series)

Book 1
Book 2
Book 3
Book 4

Girls Who Belong To Other Men (2 book series)

Book 1
Book 2

Opening Pandora's Box (5 book series)

Book 1: Jessie Plays For Her Husband
Book 2: Ollie Watches His Wife With Another Man
Book 3: Jessie Grows Closer To Roman
Book 4: Jessie Loses Herself In Roman
Book 5: How Can You Do This To Me?

Available at Amazon Kindle and Smashwords.

CHAPTER 1

Getting invited to the ultra exclusive party had been easier than Ollie thought it would be. Though it took some sleuthing on Google to find it. He sent an email, and after a short back and forth with the host, directions to the party were sent to him. The deal was sealed when he emailed to the host a picture of Jessie in a bikini from the previous summer.

Jessie nervously fidgeted in the car. "I can't believe I let you talk me into this," she said nervously. "A swinger's party! I swear Ollie, if you're doing this just so you can get into some girl's pants, I'm going to strangle you!"

Ollie chuckled and squeezed his wife's hand. "You know that's not what this is about," he said reassuringly. He'd explained everything to her earlier. This party wasn't for swingers, not really. Two types of people were invited, married couples and "bulls." The purpose, of course, was for the bulls to fuck the wives while their husbands watched. The bulls were young, handsome, well hung muscular guys, almost all black. Ollie had made it clear to the host they were going just to watch this time, and probably wouldn't participate. The host wasn't bothered at all by this, especially after seeing Jessie's picture.

After the drama with Roman had been taken care of, Jessie had finally told Ollie what happened with Lorenzo, and how she'd almost gotten fucked. Ollie was beside himself with excitement and fucked her non-stop that night, making her tell him over and over again what happened. Afterwards, he felt jealous and bothered that she'd let things get that far. In fact, it sounded to him like she would have let Lorenzo fuck her except Roman had stepped in. Still, he couldn't stop thinking about it and part of him wished she'd fucked Lorenzo. He thought this party would be a good next step, and talked Jessie into going. It took a while of cajoling, but finally she agreed to go.

They were met at the door by the host, who lecherously looked Jessie up and down (she looked stunning in a black strapless cocktail dress) and invited them to tour the house. They went into the kitchen to get a drink. On the way, they ran into two bulls. In greeting they each lightly kissed Jessie's hand and asked if she wanted to party. She politely declined but Ollie could tell she was excited by the atmosphere. The bulls were cool about it and kissed Jessie on the cheek, making sure to press their erections against her stomach (they were both nude except for tiny Speedos). "Maybe we'll see you later," they said. "Maybe," Jessie replied a little shyly. She had to admit to herself, the men were handsome and it was a thrill to be getting so much attention.

In the kitchen, a large black man was fucking a cute brunette on the kitchen counter. A tall handsome white man stood next to them, his dick in his hand as he watched the bull fuck his wife. The bull caught sight of Jessie and immediately said, "I'll be done in a minute if you wanna dance."

"Thanks, but we're just, um ... looking around," Jessie said nervously, not knowing what to do with her eyes because he was stark naked. And he was fucking a pretty white girl. In the freaking kitchen.

The bull grinned a friendly smile. "That's cool," he said while still fucking the brunette. "If you don't mind me saying, you've got great legs. Are you wearing a garter belt?"

Jessie hesitated – it seemed strange to carry out a conversation with him while he was having sex with another girl – but then she nodded. The bull asked "can I see?" In a weird way his request seemed normal given the circumstances, so Jessie raised her skirt revealing her lacy stocking tops and garter belt straps.

"Very nice," the bull said admiringly. The brunette's husband thought so too as he shifted his gaze from his wife getting fucked, to Jessie's legs. "Maybe we can get to know each other later," the bull said.

"Maybe," Jessie said. She pushed down her skirt. Her cheeks were flushed.

They poured themselves drinks and left the kitchen. The husband caught up with Ollie and Jessie. "I'm Victor," the husband said, offering his hand. Ollie hesitated knowing where his hand had been a moment ago, but then realized he was being ridiculous and shook the man's hand. "I'm Ollie, this is my wife Jessie."

"That's my wife Jacky in there, with Tyrone." Victor was a tall muscular guy himself, and his penis (which was still erect and hanging out of his pants) was an impressive size. He could have been a bull himself (albeit a white one). Victor didn't try to hide his attraction to Jessie. "Sometimes we swing with other couples. We'd love to get together with you, you're incredibly beautiful."

Jessie didn't know how to respond, and Victor took Jessie's silence as acquiescence. He leaned closer and palmed her thigh. "Tyrone is right, you have fantastic legs."

Jessie gulped as she felt Victor's hand move under her skirt and caress her thigh. She tensed as his fingertips passed her lacy stocking tops and moved onto her soft bare skin above. She looked at Ollie, but he made no move to stop Victor. His eyes were on her skirt, which was creased with Victor's hand underneath it. Jessie looked back at Victor, and he smiled at her as he caressed the tender flesh above her stocking tops.

At that moment, they heard Jacky call Victor's name in the throes of passion. "I better be going," he said. He leaned in and kissed Jessie. She opened her lips, allowing his tongue into her mouth. As they French kissed, Victor moved his hand between their bodies and fondled her breast, and Jessie let him. Jacky screamed again and Victor reluctantly pulled away. "Remember my offer," he said, leaving Jessie panting and Ollie so hard it hurt.

The married couple looked at each other, both more aroused than ever before. They both gulped down their drinks.

"This place is wild," Ollie said.

"Yeah," Jessie agreed, her cheeks still flushed. "I feel like I'm back at Penn State."

"Really? Your sorority had parties like this?"

"No, not Triple D," Jessie replied. She'd been a member of the Delta-Delta-Delta (or Tri Delta) sorority in college. "But the frats got wild sometimes."

Ollie slowly nodded, taking this in. He'd met Jessie when she was a junior. She'd been uber popular back then. She still was. He'd been a geeky math grad student. And he still was – geeky.

To this day, it still amazed him they got together and fell in love. Especially that she'd fallen in love with him. But then opposites attract.

Ollie was always fascinated about hearing about her life before they met. And also insecure about her life back then, when she had her pick of guys and dated all the time.

He felt insecure and nervous about being at this party too. He wanted this, but he didn't. Seeing Jessie with another man – having sex with another man. It was his biggest fantasy. But at the same time, he wasn't sure if he could handle it. Still, he didn't want to leave.

They refilled their glasses – there were self-serve mini-bars all around the house. Then, Ollie took Jessie's hand and led her upstairs to continue their tour. All the bedroom doors were open, and there were naked bodies everywhere, black men on white (and married) girls. In the master bedroom, a black man was fucking a pretty red head missionary style. Three other black guys stood in line waiting their turn, all of them naked and stroking their cocks. One of the guys noticed Jessie and approached her. "I'm Jerome," he said with a movie star smile. "You must be Jessie."

Jessie's eyes got wide with surprise. "How do you know my name?" she asked.

Jerome's smile widened. "Word travels fast," he said, appreciatively looking Jessie up and down.

"So what am I? Fresh meat?" Jessie asked.

Jerome laughed. He didn't deny it. Instead, he said "At least you're still dressed." He motioned to himself. He was naked. "I had the Speedo on, but we're supposed to take it off."

"So that's your dress code?" Jessie teased with a grin.

"It's a small price to pay," Jerome said, grinning.

"To have sex with married white girls?" Jessie asked.

"Everyone's got to have a hobby," Jerome joked. They both laughed.

As Jessie flirted with Jerome, Ollie stood silent next to her. It was funny she'd mentioned frat parties moments ago, because now he felt like they were back in college. Back then, it was always like this. Jessie, the popular social butterfly that everyone wanted to talk to, and him, following her around like a puppy dog and hoping for a little of her attention.

He felt like a third wheel. And the feeling was disturbing ... and thrilling.

"So how do you like the party?" Jerome asked.

"It's ... interesting," she said, again not knowing where to direct her eyes with the black man being completely nude and his big hard cock pointing straight at her.

"That's Sally on the bed, with Toby," Jerome said pointing at the bed, like a sports announcer doing play-by-play. As he spoke, he put his arm around Jessie's waist.

"That's Rich over there, Sally's husband." Rich sat a few feet from the bed, stroking himself as he watched Toby fuck his wife. In contrast to Victor, Rich looked the part of a cuckold husband. Balding, paunchy gut, his fingers wrapped around a small dick. He looked so different from his wife Sally. She looked to be mid-40s and attractive, with big perfect breasts and long legs that ended in black stiletto high heels.

"Sally's insatiable," Jerome continued, caressing Jessie's back. "She can't get enough."

"I see that," Jessie replied seeing the line of bulls and feeling Jerome's fingers slowly tracing up her side.

Jerome understood Jessie's meaning and laughed. "Oh, me and my boys aren't waiting our turn. We're letting Toby warm Sally up, then we'll join in. Sally likes to be completely filled. If you get what I'm saying."

"Oh," Jessie said softly, the idea of Sally taking on all 4 black men at the same time sinking in. She could imagine where three of them would go, but what would the fourth one do? The possibilities made her shudder and she gulped down her drink.

She forgot about Jerome for a moment. But then she felt his fingers trail up the side of her breast. Still watching Sally and Toby, Jerome cupped Jessie's breast with his large hand.

"This alright with you?" Jerome asked, smiling at Ollie as he continued to cup and caress Jessie's small breast. Hearing her husband's name, Jessie turned to look at him. For a moment, she'd forgotten he was there.

Ollie looked frozen in place. He managed to nod his head yes. Jerome winked at Ollie and then Jessie felt him rub her nipple between his thumb and finger through the thin material of her dress (she hadn't worn a bra). Her eyelids fluttered and her lips parted in a soft O.

"Ollie, Jessie's glass is empty," Jerome said authoritatively. "Get her a refill, will you? I could use one myself."

It bothered Ollie at being ordered around by Jerome, especially in front of his wife. But his face felt hot with excitement. "What are you drinking?" he heard himself ask.

"Red bull, what else," he said with a chuckle. "With a shot of vodka."

Ollie felt shamed walking out of the bedroom and leaving his wife with Jerome. Sally's husband gave him an understanding look, which didn't make Ollie feel better. In fact it made him sick. He might have fantasies about his wife with other men, but he wasn't a pathetic cuckold like Rich. And he certainly didn't want Jessie to see him that way.

In the kitchen, Ollie was approached by 2 handsome black men. They were naked, had muscular bodies like NFL linebackers, and cocks that ran down their thighs like pythons. "Are you Jessie's husband?" one of them asked. When Ollie nodded, they shook his hand. "I'm Kelvin and this is Jamal. We'd love to get together with her. There's room in the playroom right now. "

Clearly word of his beautiful wife had gotten around the entire house. Ollie wasn't surprised. Of the girls he'd seen in the house, Jessie was by far the prettiest, and one of the youngest. "She's upstairs right now," Ollie said without thinking, his head fogged with lust.

"Thanks for the tip!" Deion said, slapping Ollie on the back and taking his words as an invitation. He and Jamal ran up the stairs.

Ollie made the drinks. Part of him wanted to rush back upstairs to protect his wife. But another part – a big part – wanted to see what would happen. So he took his time making the drinks. And he took his time walking up the stairs.

When he got there, he saw that more men had crowded into the bedroom. There must have been a dozen or more. Ollie had to squeeze in.

Jessie was sandwiched between Jerome and another naked black man – his name was Stefon. Other than Toby who was still on the bed with Sally, all the other men were watching the action with Jessie, including Sally's husband.

All of them had their cocks out, stroking themselves. It looked like Toby was still inside Sally, but he was no longer fucking her. Instead he was watching the action with Jessie. Even Sally was looking at Jessie, annoyed at all the attention she was getting.

Jerome faced Jessie, and they were locked in a deep open mouth kiss. From their cheeks, Ollie could tell Jerome's tongue was inside Jessie's mouth. Jessie's skirt was bunched up around her waist. Jerome's hands cupped and squeezed her tight ass cheeks. The man behind her, Stefon, was kissing her neck, and his hands were on her breasts (which were amazingly still inside the bodice of her strapless dress). Ollie gulped down the Red Bull and vodka.

Jerome began nudging Jessie to the bed, and Stefon followed suit. While locked in their embrace, the three slowly moved toward the bed. Toby ungraciously pulled Sally off the bed, making room for his black brothers and the pretty blonde. Sally yelled "Hey!" but no one paid any attention to her, not even her husband. The other black men closed in around the trio, stroking their cocks and waiting their turn.

Within moments, Jessie was lying on the bed. Jerome was in front, still kissing her. Stefon was pressed against her back. He pulled the front of her dress down, exposing her small breasts. Jessie groaned into Jerome's mouth as Stefon squeezed and rubbed her hard, naked nipples.

Jerome and Stefon acted as a team. Stefon put his hand under Jessie's knee and raised her shapely leg. This exposed and opened her up for Jerome. Jerome hurriedly rolled a condom onto his shaft, then took his cock into his hand and positioned himself. He got into position to penetrate Jessie's pussy with his big black cock.

Ollie knew this was it, he was about to see his sweet faithful wife fucked at last, and not just by one man but by many men, all of them black with huge cocks, and they would violate all her holes. He felt ready to cum in his pants.

But then something snapped inside. He moved forward and grabbed Jessie, pulling her away from Jerome and Stefon.

Jessie's pretty blue eyes were glazed over and her cheeks flushed. "What, what?" she softly said disoriented, as if coming out of a daze.

"We're leaving," Ollie announced, pushing Jessie's skirt down and fixing the top to cover her naked breasts. He looked around. They were surrounded by a lot of big muscular black men, and he wondered if they'd be allowed to leave.

Jerome sensed Ollie's concern and laughed. "Shit man, what do you think this is?" He looked disappointed but waved to the door, indicating they were free to leave whenever they wanted. Ollie grabbed his wife's arm and pulled her out of the room.

CHAPTER 2

Ollie and Jessie had barely spoken the last 2 weeks. Ollie didn't know what to say. His emotions were so mixed he frustrated himself, so he was certain his wife must be exasperated if not infuriated with him.

Also, it bothered him Jessie let all those men fondle her, and seemed ready to let them fuck her. They'd agreed ahead of time they were just going to watch, but Jessie seemed ready to do much more than that, to let them gangbang her. What had happened to his sweet, church going wife?

Jessie was furious at her husband. She felt like he was jerking her around, cajoling her to do things, then changing this mind at the last second. He made her feel guilty, like this was all her idea, which was completely unfair because he was the one who started all this.

"I'm done with this stupid game of yours! Don't ever ask me to do anything like that again!" she'd said angrily when he'd asked how she could have let the black bulls get so far with her.

It WAS completely unfair. Ollie was putting her in these situations, how could she not get aroused? But then he made her feel like it was all her fault.

At the same time, a part of her DID feel like she was acting like a slut. She felt the same self-reproaching feelings she'd felt back in college the times she had one night stands. She didn't like feeling like that. She thought she'd gotten away from all that when she married Ollie. All she wanted was to have Ollie's babies and be a good devoted, faithful wife, and his demented fantasies were ruining everything.

Yet ... hadn't it been exciting? And fun? Like back in college, before she met Ollie, when she was young and free and could flirt and party all she wanted. The way Jerome and Stefon so clearly desired her, and Tony and Nicholas, and … and …

God! There were so many men she couldn't remember all their names! And that was … wicked … thrilling.

Still not talking to each other, Ollie and Jessie entered church and immediately ran into Roman and the kids. Roman looked terrible. "What's wrong?" Jessie asked concerned.

Roman sent the kids ahead and then quietly said, "Alicia left me last night."

"Oh no!" Jessie said startled. "That's horrible!"

Roman and Alicia's breakup seemed to snap Ollie and Jessie out of their funk. Ollie apologized for making Jessie feel like a slut. It turned him on when she acted that way. He assured her she'd done only what he asked, so if there was any blame it was all on him. He said the party had been too much all at once. In his fantasies, Jessie was with just one guy, not multiple men like at the party.

Ollie admitted he felt jealous and insecure whenever they played the game. But somehow, those feelings just added to his excitement. But having so many big black naked guys hitting on her all at the same time had just been too much.

Ollie had never before been so open with his feelings about the game – about anything really. While incredibly sweet and caring, her husband was shy and an introvert, and wasn't the best at revealing what he was feeling inside.

His opening up softened Jessie, and she opened up too. She admitted she'd been terribly excited, and the taboo of having sex with a black man had always intrigued her. Also, all the attention she'd gotten had thrilled her. But when he pulled her away she'd actually been relieved. She had never been with more than one man, and never with a black man. Having so many men surrounding her – big, naked, black men—had been too much.

Jessie ended by calling Ollie her hero for pulling her out of that situation, and they kissed and hugged.

They made passionate sex all night, re-living the party with their pillow talk and role playing. Ollie purposely didn't ask if she would've actually fucked the black men if he had let her. He didn't want to hear her answer.

Two weeks later the phone rang. It was Roman. "I'm sorry to ask this, but I don't know who else to call. Emma fell down and I think she might have broken her arm. Can you or Ollie watch the other kids while I take her to the ER?"

"Of course, I'll be right over!" Jessie said concerned. On the way over she called Ollie to let him know what happened (he was traveling for work again).

Roman was away for about 3 hours, and luckily Emma's arm wasn't broken, just bruised. When he got home he looked stressed, so Jessie found a bottle of wine in his cabinet and poured for both of them. "Have you heard from Alicia?" she asked.

Roman nodded looking sullen. "She moved in with one of her old boy friends."

"Oh Roman I'm so sorry!"

He shrugged. "Maybe it's for the best. We haven't been getting along well. Mostly I worry about the kids."

The next day, Jessie couldn't stop thinking about Roman. He had to take care of their 3 kids all by himself. While there last night, she'd looked into his refrigerator and pantry and there wasn't much food inside. Ollie was still traveling and it was a slow day at work, so she left early and went to the grocery store. She loaded two shopping carts and went over to Roman's.

"What's this?" Roman said opening the door.

Jessie stood smiling with groceries in her arms. "I just thought you could use some help. There's more in the car."

Roman said she shouldn't have, but he looked grateful. While Roman brought in the bags, Jessie made spaghetti. Afterwards she helped him give the kids baths and put them to bed. "Thanks a lot for this," he said looking embarrassed. "I've hired a nanny, but she hasn't started yet."

"I'm glad to help," she said sitting down and crossing her long legs. Roman looked at her legs, but she pretended not to notice. He opened a bottle of wine and poured them each a glass. She'd told him she was a dancer, and he believed it. She had the slim yet athletic body of a dancer, her posture was classically perfect, and all her movements were graceful. Even walking across the room she looked like she was dancing. She also was the most beautiful girl he'd ever met.

"Do you mind?" Jessie said taking the remote control.

Roman laughed when Jessie turned the cable to ESPN. "Are you kidding?"

Jessie smiled. "I told you I had 3 older brothers." They watched Sports Center in silence for a while.

"Are you going to church on Sunday?" Roman asked.

"Um ... I'm not sure," Jessie replied, caught off guard by the non-sequitur. She hadn't planned to go because Ollie wasn't getting home until Monday.

"I think I'll take the kids," Roman said. "I think routine will help. With Alicia being gone."

"Oh yeah, you're probably right," Jessie said. At that moment she knew she would go. She wanted to help with the kids. But the idea of seeing Roman again excited her.

Jessie thought about telling Ollie her plans, but decided not to. She knew what his reaction would be – he'd want her to flirt with Roman – and she didn't want that. Roman was clearly hurting, and stressed about suddenly being thrown into single parenthood. And anyways, he and Alicia weren't divorced, just separated.

Sunday morning, she had trouble deciding what to wear. She'd teased Roman before in church, when they first met. But that was before she knew him, when he was just a hunky guy and she was playing a harmless game of seeing if she could get his attention. She'd always been a flirt, and it was a harmless game she played sometimes. But now she knew Roman, they were friends, and he was going through a lot. Still .... she smiled impishly. She opened her drawer and picked out a garter belt and stockings, and started dressing.

At church she found Roman standing next to the door. He was talking to the pastor, but she wondered if he was waiting for her. As always, she took Emma in her lap (her arm was in a sling but not broken).

She made sure to "accidentally" flash her stocking tops at Roman during the service. She'd carefully picked out her dress. It was made of a dark silky material, and sitting next to her, Roman would be able to easily see the dents in the filmy material formed by her hard nipples (she hadn't worn a bra), but farther away no one would notice. She felt terribly sinful teasing Roman in church, so she prayed to God for forgiveness, even while at the same time the delicious wickedness made her nipples even harder.

Roman looked repeatedly at her legs and chest. She pretended not to notice. After service, Roman invited her over to watch football. She felt sorry for him. She knew it would help him out if she went over and helped with the kids. She agreed to meet him later, after she changed and picked up some food.

At home, she called Ollie but still didn't tell him about Roman. Sure, she was teasing Roman a little, but that was just her flirting like she often did. It was all harmless, and she didn't want Ollie to go crazy about it.

She took off her outfit until she was down to her thong. She pulled on black tights because it was cold outside. She usually wore tights or pantyhose under jeans during the winter. Then she put on a bra, jeans and a Penn State sweatshirt. She looked in the mirror. It was an okay outfit for an afternoon of watching football, but ....

Reconsidering, she pulled off the sweatshirt and found a light brown turtleneck that looked good with her blonde hair. She was about to put on the turtleneck when she glanced at herself in the mirror. Her bra was smooth and full coverage. She liked it because under the turtleneck it wouldn't show any lines. But on impulse, she took off the bra and replaced it with a heavily laced, unlined bra.

She put on the turtleneck and looked at herself in the mirror. As she knew it would, the texture of the lace showed through the snug turtleneck. The fashion gurus at Glamour magazine wouldn't approve, but she knew men found it alluring to see the lines of a girl's bra. The unlined bra also made her breasts look natural, and would do nothing to mask her nipples if they got hard. She fleetingly thought about wearing high heels, but thought that too much, and slipped into her black, pointy toe Mia flats.

At Roman's, Jessie made chicken fingers, fries and tacos. They played board games with the kids. Jessie loved being around kids and had a great time, even with the TV locked on football all day long (despite what she said, she didn't really like watching football if it wasn't Penn State).

After dinner, Jessie helped Roman give the kids baths and put them to sleep. Jessie felt Roman's eyes constantly on her. She wasn't wearing her tightest skinny jeans, but the designer 7 For All Mankind jeans she wore were tight enough. Anyways, she looked at him a lot as well (he looked good in his jeans too), although she felt she was better at sneaking peaks at him, than he at her.

Roman poured Jessie a glass of wine and opened a beer for himself. They talked more about Penn State, and realized they used to go to the same haunts. Before long, they were talking about everything, laughing and having a good time. Jessie had a hole in her jeans, and at one point

Roman playfully poked her knee through the hole. "Can't afford new jeans?" he joked.

Jessie pretended to be hurt. "It costs a lot to buy jeans with holes," she said with a pretend pout.

She expected him to laugh at her joke and remove his finger, but he didn't. Instead, he brushed his finger back and forth over the nylon. "You wear pantyhose under your jeans?"

"Um, tights actually," she said feeling awkward talking about her underwear and realizing he probably didn't know the difference between tights and pantyhose.

"It's cold outside," she explained pulling her leg away. An awkward silence followed. Jessie liked to flirt, but she could tell when flirting went from harmless to dangerous, and they were close to that point now.

She pulled her legs underneath her, trying to think of a way to change the subject. As she did her flats fell off her feet and hit the floor. Roman's head jerked and he gawked at her stocking clad feet. "Shit, he has a foot fetish, just like Ollie" she thought realizing things were going from bad to worse. Trying to be as unsexy as possible, she sat back up and primly slipped her flats back on. "Um, is there any more wine?" she asked holding her empty glass and trying to change the subject.

Other than that one awkward moment, they both had a great time, talking and laughing about everything. Finally Jessie looked at the clock and her eyes widened. "It's past midnight! I've got to get home, I have to go to work early tomorrow!"

Roman gave her a hug goodbye and then kissed her cheek. It looked like he was going to kiss her on the lips, so she quickly pulled away and left.

The next day Ollie got home, and in bed Jessie told him what had happened. Ollie got excited and made her put on exactly what she'd worn the night before. He rubbed her nipples so he could see what Roman had seen. He stood behind her as Roman had done as she pretended to wash the dishes, so he could see her tight shapely ass the way Roman had.

Over and over again he made her describe how Roman had caressed her knee, and then he put his finger through the hole saying, "like this, he touched you like this?" He went wild when she described Roman's reaction to when her flats fell off. "You shouldn't have put them back on!" he chastised her. Finally he peeled off her jeans and ripped a hole in her tights. "The next time you see Roman I want you to wear these pantyhose!" he hissed as he plunged his cock into her.

"You want me to see him again?" she whimpered as he fucked her.

"Yes!" Ollie lustfully growled. "Next time I want you to tease him until he's cumming in his pants." He grabbed Jessie's jeans and ripped the hole larger. "See? I'm helping you seduce him. He'll love seeing more of sexy legs in hose!" Ollie grabbed Jessie's hair and pulled her head to the side, then he plunged his tongue into her ear.

"Ugh god," Jessie cried. For some reason her ears had always been super sensitive, so sensitive that when Ollie did this it actually hurt. Ollie knew this so he did it only when he was completely out of control with lust. "Ollie don't," she pleaded, grimacing at the pleasure/pain.

"You slut! You dress like a slut and go over there and tease him like a slut. But then you don't even given him a hand job! You're a cock teasing slut! Admit it you're a cock tease!"

"Yes, I'm a slut!" Jessie agreed, but at this point she just wanted Ollie to cum so he would pull his tongue out of her ear. "I'm a slut! I purposely dressed like a slut to turn Roman on! I took off my shoes so he could see my feet! I wiggled my toes in my tights right in front of his face! I got him hard but I didn't go down on him or let him fuck me because I'm a slutty tease!"

"Just like at the party, right? You got all those black guys hot but then you didn't fuck them—you didn't even touch their cocks did you? Did you? No, because you're just a cock tease!"

"Yeah, yeah, that's right!" Jessie pleaded as Ollie repeatedly darted his tongue into her ear. "Ollie, please stop ..."

"You're a cock tease, a slutty cock tease! Just like tonight! You teased Roman, you slut, didn't you? But you didn't give it up, did you, you slutty cock tease?"

"Yeah, yeah, I'm a cock tease, yeah!" Jessie felt her husband's body tense, and then he finally came. As they lay panting, Jessie wondered what had just happened. She hadn't cum, and it seemed Ollie didn't seem to care. Instead, he'd done something he knew she hated. In a way she felt violated.

But, he'd been away for a week, and then he'd gotten so excited about what had happened with Roman. Maybe his passions got the better of him. She felt confused but she missed him, so she snuggled into his arms and fell asleep.

Ollie felt chipper the next day. Their sex last night had been fantastic, and he couldn't stop thinking about what had happened with Roman.

The next Sunday, they went to church, but to Ollie's disappointment they weren't able to sit next to Roman because his pew was full. Jessie didn't wear a skirt, but a blouse and slim pants that made her ass and legs look fantastic. After the service, Ollie and Jessie got caught in the crowd, and Roman and his kids were gone by the time they got to the door. The pastor hurried past, looking around. "Have you seen Roman?" he asked holding up a diaper bag. "I think this is his."

"Oh, it is," Jessie said recognizing the bag immediately. She took it from the pastor. "We'll bring it to him."

They drove a couple of miles towards Roman's house when Ollie pulled over. "Why don't you go over to Roman's place on your own?" he said, a mischievous grin on his face.

At first Jessie didn't understand but then it hit her. "Ollie, you're insatiable," she said a playful smile coming to her pretty face.

This was something Ollie loved about Jessie. She was carefree and always up for an adventure. "I'll take a taxi home," he said. "But take your time, as much time as you want, even dinner with him. You can tell Roman I had to go to the office."

Jessie shook her head like she couldn't believe her husband's one track mind. But still she wore a smile. "You're crazy, you know that?"

Ollie leaned towards her and whispered hotly into her ear. "Take off your bra first," he said as he began unbuttoning her blouse.

Alarmed, Jessie's eyes darted around. "Ollie, stop, people will see!"

His grin grew wider. "So hurry up and take it off," he teased.

Jessie thought about it. Her blouse was silky and a dark cream color. The dark of her nipples and areola probably wouldn't show through if she was careful where she stood. If her nipples got hard they would poke through the silky material but she'd done worse things. Also, she knew Ollie wouldn't stop until she took off her bra. So she did a Flashdance move and took off her bra without taking off her blouse, teasingly putting on a sultry face but then giggling. "You are so demented!" she said playfully to her husband, dramatically dropping her bra in his lap.

"I've got something for you," he said putting the bra in his pocket and reaching into the glove compartment. He pulled out 3 square packages. Jessie immediately saw they were condoms. "Just in case," he explained. "You know Roman has 3 kids, so clearly he's very fertile. And you're not on any birth control now, right?"

Jessie hesitated. Then she said "No, I'm not" without taking her eyes off the square packages. She'd gone off the pill a few months ago. They both wanted to start a family soon (probably her more than Ollie), so they decided to let nature take its course.

"So, we're really doing this?" Jessie asked her husband.

"If you want."

"No Ollie, this can't be just on me," Jessie said. "You have to want this to happen too."

"Does that mean you want it to happen?" he asked.

Jessie hesitated, then said "I don't know. Once I do this – if I do it – we can't go back. And, I mean, Roman is still married to Alicia. He'd be cheating."

"Alicia's living with her old boyfriend," Ollie reminder her. "You think she's not having sex? And anyway, the idea of you getting another man to cheat on his wife is a major turn on."

"Oh my god Ollie, that is seriously evil," Jessie said.

Ollie laughed. He dropped the condoms into her purse and kissed her cheek. "I'll see you at home later," he said getting out of the car. "I hope you have good stories to tell me."

Thirty minutes later, Jessie knocked on Roman's door. "Hey!" he said clearly pleased to see her.

"Hi," she replied smiling. She held up the diaper bag. "You left this at church."

"Thanks!" he said gratefully, relief on his face. "But you didn't have to come all this way."

"That's okay, Ollie had to go to the office."

"Well, come on in," he said enthusiastically. Jessie stepped in, being careful where she stood because if the sunlight hit her profile, Roman would get an eyeful of her braless breasts through her blouse.

She suddenly became aware of what Roman was wearing. Or not wearing really, because all he had on was a white bath towel around his waist. He had a smaller towel in his hand which he used to rubbed his wet hair. Clearly he'd just got out of the shower.

"Oh, I'm sorry, you're getting ready to go somewhere," she said turning to leave.

"No, no, don't go yet, let me get you a soda," he said. He got a Coke from the refrigerator.

"Um, do you have a Coke Zero?"

Roman looked again. "I've got Diet Pepsi, Pepsi Max and Diet Coke."

Jessie scrunched up her face. "That's okay, I'll just have ice water."

Roman opened his hands in a "what the heck?" gesture. "They're all the same," he said grinning.

"No they're not."

Roman laughed. "They're all diet soda, they all taste the same."

Jessie crossed her arms stubbornly. She hated being disagreed with. "You're wrong," she said with finality.

Roman kept smiling but decided to drop it. He was getting to know her, and knew she had a stubborn streak and a quick temper. He found it all charming though, and it didn't hurt that she looked so damn cute when she got angry.

As Roman fiddled with ice and water, Jessie took the opportunity to look him up and down. She liked what she saw. Dark complexion, a well-defined chest, broad shoulders and muscular arms and legs. Very tall. Soft dark hair ran from below his belly button to around his biceps, and the sight made her shiver (Ollie's chest was almost hairless).

She looked away just before he turned with the ice water, pretending to study the pictures on the shelves. "Why do you keep pictures of all your old girl friends?" Jessie noticed they all looked like Alicia: curvy with big chests and short dark hair.

"I don't know," he shrugged, "I guess that's just how I am. I like to remember my past."

"But didn't Alicia get mad?"

"Yeah, sometimes, but I always told her it was okay with me if she put up pictures of her old boyfriends." Jessie thought that strange but didn't say anything more, although she didn't see any pictures of Alicia with her old boyfriends.

Just then the phone rang. He saw the caller ID and looked apologetic. "I'll just be a minute," he said picking up the phone. As he looked away, she snuck a look at his crotch and saw what appeared to be a thick snake outlined in the towel. She remembered Harper's measuring technique. At least two hands, she thought with a smile. Maybe two and a half.

"Alicia just picked up the kids," Jessie heard Roman say to the person on the phone. She couldn't make out what the person on the other end of the line was saying, but she was certain it was a woman's voice. "That's great. I can't wait to see you too. Bye."

"Alicia's back?" Jessie asked, processing what she'd just heard.

Roman nodded. "Just got back last week. We saw a judge this week and worked out joint custody."

"So, what, you're going out on a date?" Jessie asked, a fake smile planted on her pretty face but her question coming out like an accusation.

"Well ... yeah," Roman said warily, noticing Jessie's sudden coldness. Then he added flippantly, "I mean, life goes on."

"Life ... goes ... on," Jessie slowly repeated as if analyzing every word.

"Well, have a good time," she said tersely, walking towards the door. Then on impulse she impishly paused in front of the window next to the door, pretending to look in her purse for her car keys and turning slightly to show Roman her profile. With the bright sun making her blouse almost transparent, she knew her braless, perky breasts and upturned nipples were clearly visible for Roman to see. She got some satisfaction when, out of the corner of her eye, she saw him trying to hide a growing hard-on.

Jessie opened the door and was startled to see a young woman standing on the stoop. "Oh," the girl said just as surprised to see Jessie. She was younger than Jessie, and very pretty. Like Alicia and Roman's old girlfriends, she had short dark hair and a classic hour glass figure with very big breasts. Jessie's minor victory over teasing Roman with a flash of her breasts was short lived when she saw the huge chest of Roman's date. "Does Roman live here?" the girl asked.

"Yes, he's inside," Jessie replied feeling awkward. For some reason she felt the need to explain why she was there. "We go to the same church. He left something there and I just brought it to him." She flushed with embarrassment and hurriedly added, "Anyways, I'm leaving now, goodbye."

"Jessie wait," Roman said stepping onto the stoop. "Bianca, can you wait inside? I just need to talk to Jessie for a minute."

Bianca looked chagrined and flashed Roman a petulant inquiringly look (he was still wearing just a towel around his waist), but she stepped into the house. Roman closed the door and turned to Jessie. "Are you okay?"

"I'm fine," Jessie snapped, her short temper flaring up. "Roman, you're freaking standing in a towel and your date is waiting. Don't you think you should go back inside?"

"Wait," Roman said grabbing her arm. "You never told me why you came by. I mean, not just to return the diaper bag?"

"I told you," Jessie said impatiently. "Ollie had to go to the office, so I thought we could hang out, maybe watch the football game or something."

Roman's face brightened. "That sounds great!" he said enthusiastically. "Come back in!"

Jessie looked at him like he was crazy. "Hello? Bianca?"

"Don't worry about that, I'll get rid of her," he said immediately. "Don't give me that look, I'll make up a good excuse like I have to pick up the kids or something." He leaned in and whispered conspiratorially. "To be honest, I think she's too young for me."

Jessie rolled her eyes. "Ya think?!" she scoffed. She scowled at him. "Anyways, you can't do that Roman, it would really be a dick move."

Just then they heard a car horn. "Hey Jessie is that you?" Jessie turned and saw it was her friend Harper from work. She glanced worriedly at Roman and then ran over to Harper's car.

"What are you doing here?" Jessie asked.

"What are you?" Harper replied, then looked over her designer Gucci sunglasses at Roman who was still standing on the stoop, obviously waiting for Jessie to come back. "And who is your friend over there? What's his name, Mr. Hunk?"

Jessie knew what Harper must be thinking. "That's Roman, he's from church, and has 3 kids," she quickly blurted out. She grimaced inside knowing she probably sounded guilty.

"I see," Harper said overly dramatically, drawing out the I. "And his wife?"

"They're separated."

"I see," Harper repeated, again drawing out the I like she was Sherlock Holmes and had just heard an important clue to a mystery. "And where is Ollie?"

"Um ... he's at work."

"Aaahhhhh ... I see," she said as if she'd just figured out whodunit.

Jessie grimaced. The last thing she needed was for Harper to blab about this at work. She was the biggest gossip. "I know Roman from church," she said again. "He left his diaper bag at church. I brought it to him. That's all. In fact, his date is in his house. And I'm leaving."

Harper looked disappointed. "He has a girlfriend?"

"See you later," Jessie shouted to Roman, waving her hand. Roman looked disappointed as she got into her car and drove away.

"How'd it go?" Ollie asked when she walked in the door. He was disappointed she was home so early.

"Come on," Jessie said grabbing his arm. Entering their bedroom, she pushed him onto the bed. She took off her high heels and then her pants.

Ollie smiled as his wife straddled his chest. "So you had fun with Roman?"

"Shut up," she snapped, pinning his arms with her knees. "This is what you like, isn't it?" she hissed ripping a hole in her pantyhose. "You want this?" she taunted pulling her panties to the side revealing her wet pussy. "Lick me," she ordered, lowering herself on his face.

She rolled her head back as Ollie tongued her clit. The meeting at Roman's had been humiliating. She'd made a fool of herself, practically throwing herself at Roman and then finding out he had a date. She'd acted like an idiot prancing around Roman's house and giving him a peek at her small tits, when clearly what he wanted was the double Ds of Bianca. She felt so foolish.

But god, he looked so good in that towel. He got her so hot. Just being in the same room with him made her skin tingle. But she'd never been so embarrassed or felt so rejected opening the door and seeing Bianca, and it had all been Ollie's fault.

He was the one pushing her to do these things, and she decided in the car she was going to make him pay. So she grabbed his hair tight so it hurt and rubbed her pussy against his mouth. "Yeah, yeah, yeah," she moaned. Ollie had always been good at eating pussy. The best ever. She clamped Ollie's head between her strong dancer's thighs, and roughly rubbed her cunt over his face, moving his head where she wanted by roughly pulling his hair, not caring whether it hurt. "Yes!" she grunted as she came grinding hard on Ollie's face.

She rolled off Ollie and saw the confused look on his face. She immediately felt bad. It wasn't his fault. Yes, he was pushing her to do things, but she was a willing participant, more than that really because she found the games terribly thrilling. She was about to mount him to give him relief – she would fuck him really good to make it up to him—when the phone rang. She was about to ignored it, but saw it was Harper. She decided to talk to her, to head off Harper blabbing at work and starting rumors she didn't want to have to deal with.

"Okay Jessie, give me the 411, who is Roman!" Harper said as soon as Jessie answered.

Jessie was about to repeat her earlier story when she thought of a better way to make it up to her husband. She smiled slyly at Ollie and pressed the SPEAKER button on the telephone. "I told you Harper, Roman is a guy I know from church." Jessie stood up and put her heels back on, smiling at Ollie the entire time. He loved it when she pranced about in hose and high heels.

"Yeah, yeah, whatever," Harper said impatiently. "Now give me the good stuff. You said he's separated right? Usually I stay away from guys like that, because you never know, they may get back together with their wives. But Roman is SOOOOO good looking."

"Well ....," Jessie began as if deciding whether to let Harper in on a secret. She sat on the edge of the bed next to Ollie and teasingly ran a fingernail along his chest. "He used to be football player. Now he owns a gym. He works out all the time. You can really tell."

"That's what I'm saying!" Harper said excitedly. "He has an incredible chest. His biceps are soooo hard."

"Yeah, Roman has a muscular chest," Jessie cooed, teasingly poking Ollie's soft chest and biceps to emphasize the differences between him and Roman. Ollie moaned.

Jessie stood up because she didn't want Harper to hear Ollie's moans, and to prolong his torture (she knew he was loving this!). "Roman is good looking," Jessie said to Harper while looking into her husband's eyes. "Usually he has this sophisticated GQ vibe going on where he slicks his hair back. But today he just got out of the shower and his hair was all tussled like a boy."

"I know, he looked adorable!" Harper said excitedly. The she became disheartened. "But how do I snag someone as good looking as him?"

"Oh, I don't know, there are things you can do," Jessie said, moving in front of the window and showing Ollie her profile just as she'd done with Roman. Ollie gasped as his wife's perky tits became clearly visible through the blouse.

"Did you do that with Roman?" he whispered.

Jessie put her fingertip to her lips, at the same time she nodded her head yes. Ollie moaned with excitement.

Harper smiled realizing there might be something more going on between her friend and Roman. "Come on Jessie, fess up," she said intrigued. "Are you doing the nasty with Roman? Don't worry, I won't tell Ollie. I mean, most married people cheat at least once."

"Are you serious, most people cheat?" Jessie said feigning innocence, sitting back on the bed. She muted the phone and ran her fingertip along Ollie's lips. "Is that what you want, for me to cheat on you? Does that get you hot?" she whispered. "The way me getting Roman to cheat on Alisha gets you hot?"

Ollie couldn't take his eyes off his wife. He was literally panting! She was marvelous!

Jessie pulled her husband's hands to her breasts. Still muting the phone, she said, "Were you hoping Roman would touch me here?" she whispered.

"Jessie are you still there?" Harper asked. "Come on, tell me, are you having an affair?"

Jessie unmuted her iPhone and laughed merrily. "No, but it sounds like you think I should."

"Well, yeah!" Harper said. "No offense, Ollie is a nice guy, but if you have a chance to shag a man like Roman you take it! I mean, from the look of him in that towel he's probably got 3 hands going."

Jessie saw the incomprehension in Ollie's face and smiled, teasingly wrapping her hand around his erection. "I think you may be right," she giggled into the phone.

"Come on, Jessie," Harper said seriously. "Guys like that are rare. At least white guys." Harper giggled at this. "Tell me, how big is your Ollie?"

"Well ...," Jessie said with a wicked grin, squeezing her husband's cock. The head of his cock just barely cleared her fist. She said, "Ollie is about one hand."

"Oh," Harper said sympathetically. "Sorry girlfriend."

"That's okay," Jessie said cheerfully. She ran her fingertip along Ollie's lips again. "My husband has a very talented tongue."

Harper laughed and they hung up soon after.

"You are so bad," Ollie said as soon as she hung up the phone.

Jessie gave him her best sultry look. "You have no idea how bad I can be," she purred. She moved on top of him, straddling his hips. She reached down and took his cock, and lowered herself onto him.

As she began moving up and down, her mood changed. She said, "Roman has a new girlfriend. She's younger than me. And has bigger breasts."

"Your breasts are perfect," Ollie assured her. "And you have better legs. No one has better legs than you."

"I don't know ..." Jessie said, feeling uncertain. Despite her obvious beauty, she was insecure about her looks. Maybe because so much of her self-worth was tied to how she looked. And she'd always been insecure about her small breasts. She couldn't help feeling this way. Maybe because of growing up and living in the judgmental world of Instagram and Snap Chat.

"You're the most beautiful girl in the world," Ollie assured her. "I know it. And so does Roman."

Jessie couldn't help smiling. This was why she loved Ollie. He was so supportive, and considerate, and he loved her unconditionally. Ollie was her hero. That's why she married him. They were best friends. Soul mates.

Jessie wrapped her arms around her husband's neck, and they made love. For the first time in a while, they didn't talk about their game.

CHAPTER 3

Jessie fumbled with her keyboard. She couldn't concentrate. She hated her job, being an assistant to an assistant in a big multinational. Her dream had been to dance, but she'd given that up when she married Ollie. For his job – he was a math analysist in a big financial firm – he needed to be in NYC. Jessie loved NYC, but being so close to Broadway was like a bittersweet tease. Still, she was honest with herself. She was a good dancer, but not good enough for Broadway.

Jessie couldn't stop thinking about Roman and the day before. She had been teasing Ollie to get him hot when she gushed about how great a body Roman had, and how good looking he was. But really it was all true. He was sooooooo hot.

It bothered her he had a date. Hadn't he just separated from Alicia? What was he doing dating so soon? With practically a teenager no less! Jessie didn't know if she was bothered more by Bianca's age, or her big breasts.

Jessie remembered how Roman was always surrounded by girls at his gym. And at church, for that matter. Almost always, men like Roman pursued the same kind of girls— young and curvy, pretty and big breasts. It annoyed her to no end how so many men salivated over big mammary glands. Didn't they realize how gravity worked? In 10 years, Bianca's would be sagging down to her belly button, whereas her small little breasts would still be perky and perfect. And what was Roman's thing about brunettes? Didn't he know blondes had more fun?

The problem was, Roman was exactly like the hunky guys she always swooned over and dated in high school and college. That had stopped when she met Ollie, but her husband wasn't helping any with his kinky fantasies and the way he brought up Roman all the time.

The next Sunday, Jessie wore a conservative knee length dress and low-heeled shoes, as well as a full coverage bra and pantyhose. She decided she wouldn't tease Roman anymore. While she liked him a lot and wanted to continue their friendship, she thought platonic would be better.

At church, Ollie and Jessie sat next to Roman and his kids. Ollie expected to see Alicia. He'd heard she was back, and even though they were still separated, he assumed she'd attend church with her kids. But she didn't show up.

For once, Jessie didn't have Emma on her lap. Her focus seemed to be on the pastor's sermon.

But Roman's attention was on Jessie. She was stunning, and it wasn't just her outward beauty. She had an air about her, an elegant ballerina sitting in a pew. Of course, a lot of it WAS her looks. Her face was flat out gorgeous, and she regularly wore wet silky lipstick that made it hard to take your eyes off her mouth.

Her natural blonde hair was lush and long. Ollie would rather she grew it longer, but Jessie had limits because long hair was harder to deal with than short hair. So they had an inside joke, called the "bra-strap" length. During the summer, Jessie could cut her hair shorter, but it had to at least hit her bra strap. Jessie often joked, "what do you want me to do, take off my blouse so Danny can make sure not to cut above my bra strap?" Danny was her stylist, and her suggestion might be exciting except he was gay.

Ollie and Jessie had another inside joke. Her little landing strip. Jessie kept it, even though Ollie asked that she shave it off. She thought shaving it off would make her look too much like an underage teenager, which she found bothering. She smoothed things over with Ollie though, by telling him "this way you know I'm a natural blonde."

Jessie shifted and crossed her legs in the pew, and a dozen pairs of male eyes followed her movements. Ollie wondered sometimes if his wife knew her full impact on men. Sure, she noticed men looking. She was a natural flirt and liked the attention. But he doubted she noticed all the subtle male looks going her way all the time.

And then there were the little things. Like right now, with her left leg crossed over her right, Ollie watched as Jessie arched her left foot. A few times he'd seen her dangle her high heel off her toe on purpose, when she was intentionally trying to tease. But now, as she arched her foot, she wasn't doing that to tease, she probably wasn't even aware she was doing it. But seeing her pretty stocking clad foot slightly arch out of her high heel, it was delicately erotic.

Ollie noticed Roman stealing glances at his wife. Clearly Roman was captivated by her long legs and pretty feet. By the way Roman acted, Ollie could tell Jessie had him wrapped around her little finger, and the thought got him so hard it hurt. The idea of Jessie having sex with Roman – a married man – aroused him to no end. Especially if Roman and Alicia ultimately got back together, because then Roman would think of Jessie whenever he had sex with Alicia. It was an wicked thought, but Ollie couldn't help it.

———◉———

Two weeks later Ollie packed for another business trip. "Why don't you call Roman while I'm away," he said with a mischevious smile. "You could bring over dinner."

Jessie scoffed. "Ollie, I told you what happened last time. Roman likes busty teenagers. Anyways, he's our friend now. I don't want to play games with him. Real life is one thing, the game is something else and I want to keep them separate."

"Well, just think about it," he said disappearing into her closet, and then emerging a few minutes later and dropping a small bundle of clothes on the bed. "If you decide to go, wear this. Email me a picture, okay?"

Jessie rolled her eyes.

"And you still have the condoms I gave you, right?"

"Yes, I have the freaking condoms!" she said with exasperation. Ollie laughed at her reaction. An hour later, he was on the way to the airport.

Jessie tried not to think about her husband's idea, but it kept creeping into her head. Why did he have to keep pushing her with Roman? Finally, she picked up her phone but hesitated at dialing. "I'll make a casserole and bring it over. He and the kids will probably be happy to have a home cooked meal instead of Dominos again," she told herself. "I'll only stay for a little while, and just go with what I have on now. I won't change into Ollie's outfit." Satisfied with the deal she'd made with herself, she dialed Roman's number.

"Hello?" Roman answered. Jessie's heart did a flip at hearing Roman's deep masculine voice.

"Um, hi, um, it's me," she said nervously. She chided herself for sounding so idiotic and quickly added, "I mean, it's me, Jessie, you know, from church." She squeezed her eyes shut trying to control her nervousness. And god, why did she mention church? Of course he knew who she was. "Ollie just left on a trip," she finally got out, "and, well, if you and the kids aren't busy, I thought I could bring something over for dinner."

"Hey Jessie!" Roman said enthusiastically. "I'm so happy you called! This is Alicia's weekend with the kids. I was thinking about going out for dinner. Do you want to come?"

"Well, okay, yeah, I guess. Should I meet you there?"

"No, absolutely not, I'll come pick you up. No sense having 2 cars. How about at 8?"

"Um, okay, 8 is good."

"Great! Hey Jessie, I'm really glad you called. See you."

Jessie hung up the phone, feeling dumbstruck. She hadn't expected that. She got up and looked in the mirror. She had on jeans and a Penn State hoodie. She'd forgotten to ask Roman where they were going, but most likely if she didn't change she'd be underdressed wherever they went. At least, that was her excuse as she started thinking about what to change into.

She looked through what Ollie had laid out. A brown cashmere sweater, brown flared wool skirt and off-white wool cable knit tights. The outfit he selected wasn't horrible. The skirt was really short, but they'd be okay with the tights underneath. No bra or panties (how predictable!), but he'd included a lacy camisole (she'd need it because the sweater was loosely woven). He'd also picked out her brown ballet flats, the ones with satin ribbons that tied around her ankles (not what she'd have picked, but at least not 4 inch fuck me pumps).

Jessie was surprised. She thought Ollie would've picked out a sluttier outfit, but this one was, well, almost ... school girlish. Was that his intention? She knew Ollie loved it when she dressed like a high schooler. Did he want Roman to see her that way?

After showering, she put on the outfit, blow dried and brushed her hair and did her makeup, then took a picture of herself and emailed it to Ollie. "We're going out to dinner," she said in the message. "Have fun playing with little Ollie. LOL!"

"Hi" Roman said when Jessie opened the door. He gave her a quick up and down look. She couldn't read his impression. He'd probably hoped she'd wear a tight see thought top and micro mini, or something like that. Well, too bad, they were just going out as friends. She picked up her lipstick, ID and credit card, but then realized she didn't have any place to put them. She didn't want to bring a purse (she was notorious for losing things). "Could you hold these for me?" she asked, and Roman gladly took the items and put them in his pocket. Walking to his car, he opened the door for her and she slid into the car, crossing her long legs.

He drove downtown but kept getting lost, making silly wrong turns. "Are you okay?" Jessie asked.

"Yeah ... yeah," he said distracted. He found it hard to concentrate with Jessie sitting next to him dressed like she was.

"Well – you said we were going to the Starlight Club? I think you turn here."

"Oh yeah, that's right."

They parked and the maître-d led them to a table. As Roman followed Jessie his heart pounded, his eyes looking from her blonde hair to her tight ass and then down her long shapely legs. He'd never been out with a girl so beautiful. He'd seen her dressed a lot of different ways – in church and work clothes, clubbing outfits, casual jeans. But he'd never seen her like this, dressed, well, like an angel. He knew she was 25, but in this outfit she looked much younger, like an innocent coed. He pounded down 1 beer, and then another, hoping the alcohol would calm his nerves.

"Are you okay?" Jessie asked seeing him drink so fast.

He nodded, and the alcohol did help. Pretty soon they were talking and laughing about everything, just like before. Both were thoroughly enjoying each other's company.

"So how is Bianca?" Jessie asked, an impish grin on her face. "How old is she anyway? 19?"

"I'll have you know she's 20."

"Oh, that's sooooo much better," Jessie said laughing. "Seriously Roman, where do you even go to meet 20 year olds? Do you crash college frat parties? Or is your side job a dorm RA?"

"Noooo," he said acting indignant. "I met her at the gym."

"Ahhh, " Jessie said. Now that Roman mentioned it, she remembered seeing Bianca there. "Soooo ... are you dating a lot of girls from the gym?"

"A few, but I wouldn't say I'm actually dating any of them."

"Oh I get it," Jessie said with a laugh. "You're just hooking up with them."

Roman grinned awkwardly. He didn't deny it, so Jessie knew she was right.

"So what about you?" he asked wanting to change the subject. "Exactly what do you and Ollie do? He said you're not really swingers."

Jessie felt uncomfortable talking about it, but she knew turnabout was fair play. "I don't know," she started nervously. "I mean, well, it's hard to describe. I mean, it's not really hard to describe, but ..." She covered her blushing face with her hands and laughed nervously. "Do we really have to talk about this?"

"Come on, tell me, what do you do?" he urged her. "Ollie watches you – to do what? How does it work?"

"Well ...," Jessie began. "Usually I just sit alone in a bar or something, and Ollie's someplace watching, and, well, guys come up to me."

That didn't surprise Roman at all. She was gorgeous after all, but a part of him wanted to see it in action. "So show me how it works."

"What?" Jessie asked uncomprehending.

"Go to the bar over there. I'll sit some place and watch."

"You're kidding?" Jessie said, giving him a "what the fuck" look.

Roman grinned. "No, come on. I want to see for myself."

Jessie didn't like his presumptuous attitude, and felt he was making fun of her. "Well, maybe I don't want to," she said testily.

"Why not?" Roman asked challengingly. He didn't know why, but he felt bothered and angry. "Does it only work when you're dressed like a cheap whore, like that time I saw you with a guy's hand up your skirt?" He knew it was a cheap shot, and regretted it as soon as he said it, but his anger still burned so hot he didn't apologize.

Jessie's face went from shock, to hurt, to anger. "Fine," she said coldly. She held out her hand. "Can I have my lipstick please?" Roman reached into his pocket and handed the small tube to her. She fixed her lipstick, Roman's cock growing as he watched her purse her lips. He took out her credit card so she'd be able to buy drinks, but she said without emotion, "I don't need that. I never have to pay for my drinks." Without saying another word, Jessie got up and went to the bar. He saw the bouncer look her up and down and wave her in, not asking for the $60 cover charge.

Roman gave her a minute and then followed her into the bar. Unlike Jessie, he had to pay the cover.

The bar was crowded and smoky. He took a seat at a table a couple of rows away from the bar. He had a clear view of Jessie. It didn't take long before men began approaching her. She politely sent them away until a handsome dark haired man approached. She let him buy her a drink, and soon was talking and laughing with him. He offered her a cigarette, and she accepted. Roman was surprised, he didn't know Jessie smoked.

Roman watched as the man touched her as they spoke, first on her arm and hand. Then he touched her knee briefly. Jessie didn't touch him back, but she didn't stop him from touching her or pull away. Finally the man put his palm on her knee and left it there. Roman watched as he began caressing her knee, moving slowly up her thigh. Still Jessie didn't stop him. Finally when the man was an inch or so from her skirt, Jessie said something to him. The man looked disappointed and tried to change her mind, but eventually he stood up and left. Roman saw the man had a disappointed look on his face and a tent in his pants.

The man wasn't gone long enough for his stool to cool before another man took his place. Roman saw the process repeat over and over, Jessie letting the man buy her a drink, touch her up to a point, and then sending him away. He saw this happen again and again, and from the look of the crowd, other men were getting ready for their chance with the beautiful blonde. Each time it happened Roman got angrier and more bothered.

Finally, enough was enough. After the latest man left, he quickly approached. "Come on. I'll take you home," he said anger and annoyance in his voice.

Jessie gave him a dazzling smile. "Wow cowboy, you don't waste any time, do you? Shouldn't you at least buy me a drink before asking me to go home with you?"

"Come on Jessie, I'm not in the mood for games."

"Why not? Games are soooo much fun," she said with a wicked smile, running her finger along his chest. His breathing quickened at her touch. He hadn't seen her touch any of the other guys at all.

"You're drunk," Roman said noticing her slurring her words.

"Am I?" she asked teasingly. "Are you my protector? Saving me from all those men who want in my pants. I think you deserve a kiss for that." Jessie leaned over and kissed Roman's cheek, running her hands over his chest. "You're so strong. I think you can protect me," she whispered huskily into his ear.

"Jessie, come on," he said breathing hard. "Stop fucking around."

"Oops," she said softly running her finger across his cheek to rub off the lipstick she'd left. "Bianca wouldn't like that if she saw my lipstick on your cheek."

Then Jessie fixed her lipstick, taking her time, forming an O with her mouth and slowly applying the wet silky lipstick. Roman couldn't take his eyes off her mouth.

"Jessie, come on ..."

"What's wrong, is it my bobbies?" she asked with a pout, arching her back as if putting her chest on display. "I know mine aren't big like Bianca's ... or Alisha's ... or any of your old girlfriends on your shelf."

Roman stared at Jessie's chest. The weave of her sweater was so loose he could see right through to the camisole underneath. The camisole was tight and molded to her body, like a second skin over her breasts and hard nipples. Yes, they were small, but they looked so perfect and tantalizing. "Yours are fine," he said tersely.

"Do you know what Ollie likes to do? He likes me to show him how the men touched me. Would you like me to show you?" She took his hand and placed it on her knee.

"Jessie, no," he said, making as to pull his hand away, but he didn't try very hard and Jessie kept hold of his hand.

"Come on, you're the one who said you wanted to see how it worked," she said with heavy lidded eyes. She brought his hand back to her knee. With her hand over his, she ran his hand up her thigh. Through the wool tights he felt her firm, toned thighs.

"One man felt me here," she said slowly moving Roman's hand along the inside of her thigh. "Another man reached under my skirt before I stopped him." She pulled his hand underneath her skirt until his fingertips almost touched her crotch. She left his hand there. He could practically feel the heat from her pussy. Looking into his eyes, she parted her legs slightly. Not much, but just enough that he could touch her pussy if he wanted to. He felt perspiration beading on his forehead. He'd never been so turned on. It took all his will power not to move his hand further up her skirt.

She put her hand on his knee. "You know what happens next?" she whispered. She moved her hand up his leg. "Do you want to know?"

"Yes, I want to know," he said hoarsely.

Jessie smiled, pleased Roman wanted to know. Then her expression turned urgent. "After those men have touched me and gotten me so hot"—she continued slowly running her hand up his thigh—"Ollie takes me home and fucks me." She put her palm over Roman's erection, and moved it up his length.

Jessie moved closer, and whispered into his ear, "Do you want to fuck me Roman?"

Roman didn't have to be asked twice. He stood up in a flash and practically dragged Jessie from the bar. He registered the envious looks from all the men in the bar. In the car he drove home like a maniac. He was so hard he felt like he was going to burst through his pants.

Just then he felt Jessie's head in his lap. "Fuck she's so turned on, she's going down on me right here!" he thought.

He braced himself for her mouth. He knew he'd cum as soon as he felt her sexy lips around his cock. But after a few moments he realized she wasn't doing anything. "Jessie?" he asked touching her head. He didn't hear anything except her steady breathing. She'd passed out from all the alcohol.

CHAPTER 4

The next morning, Jessie woke with a wicked hangover. She took two Motrin and drank a huge cup of water. Her memory of the previous evening was spotty, but she remembered enough to be mortified by what she'd done. She had on only the camisole and tights, so somehow she'd undressed herself. Or had Roman undressed her? She shivered at the possibility.

Roman called that day and the next, but she didn't answer. Ollie got home and she told him what happened. Of course it got him turned on beyond belief and he fucked her non-stop. Afterwards to Ollie, his wife appeared reticent about it and refused to talk to Roman, either over the phone or at church.

Ollie could tell she'd been turned on, and she had been. Running her hands over Roman's hard chest and actually palming his erection had been incredibly exciting. But she had so many conflicting thoughts and feelings. Yes, it had been exciting, and she was terribly attracted to Roman. But she'd acted like a slut and it embarrassed her.

Also, she sensed Alicia wanted to get back together with Roman, so she felt like she was betraying her friend. And, she worried about Ollie and whether he could handle it if their game went much further. If their game went from fantasy to reality. She had her own mixed feelings about that, too.

But Ollie was insistent. He constantly talked to her about Roman. How he was a friend and it wasn't fair to give him the cold shoulder treatment. How he was the perfect guy to further explore their fantasies.

Ollie explained how the fantasy of her getting picked up in a bar was powerful for him, but in the end, the thought of her getting fucked by a perfect stranger wasn't something he could handle. The black bull party was the same problem, just 100 times worse. Maybe someday he'd be ready for that, but not the first time.

Roman was perfect. Clearly she was attracted to him. But also he was a friend and married (like Jessie, Ollie sensed Roman and Alicia would eventually get back together). Thus, Ollie wasn't as threatened by Roman. After weeks of being harassed and cajoled, Jessie finally agreed to meet up with Roman. "To talk, that's all," she said, agreeing with Ollie it wasn't fair to give him the cold shoulder especially after they'd become such good friends.

They invited Roman over for dinner. Ollie wanted to pick out Jessie's clothes, but she refused. Instead she picked out a turtleneck, jeans, bra, pantyhose and flats. She didn't wear makeup or even any perfume. She also wore her hair in a ponytail. Ollie's face dropped when he saw her, but he was smart enough not to say anything.

Dinner went great. It was awkward at first, but eventually the friends laughed and talked like nothing had happened. They shared two bottles of wine. Then Ollie pulled out a bottle of tequila and they did shots, laughing and giggling. "I've got a surprise," Ollie said showing them a small baggie.

Jessie looked surprised. "Is that weed?"

Ollie smiled and nodded as he rolled a joint. "I bought it from a guy at work." He lit it and took a deep drag, then handed it to Jessie.

She giggled. "Oh my god, I haven't gotten high since college!" She took a drag, holding the smoke in her lungs, then finally letting it out. "Oh my," she said, already feeling its effects.

Ollie took the joint from her and handed it to Roman. As he took a drag, Ollie turned on soft music and pulled Jessie into his arms, moving in a slow dance. Roman finished the joint and rolled another, handing it to Ollie after taking a drag. Ollie took a long drag and then so did Jessie. All three were feeling the effects of the alcohol and weed.

Ollie and Jessie continued to slowly dance, the married couple looking into each other's eyes. "What's happening?" Jessie asked with an uncertain voice.

Ollie didn't answer. He took another drag and then so did Jessie. He maneuvered Jessie to where Roman stood. With a casual grin that belied the seriousness of the moment, he handed his wife to Roman. Hesitantly, Roman put his arms around Jessie's waist. She looked at Ollie uncertainly, then looked at Roman and put her arms around his neck. They began to dance, slowly moving from side to side, looking into each other's eyes. Ollie sat in a chair, mesmerized.

Roman was rock hard. Jessie felt so good in his arms. She looked more beautiful than ever, and without makeup she looked so young, like a ripe teen model on the cover of the J-14 magazine. As they danced, he didn't smell her normal perfume. Instead, he smelled baby powder she put on after showing. He was so completely captivated by her, and looking into her face was hypnotic.

As if in a dream, Roman heard himself ask Ollie, "May I kiss your wife?"

Ollie gulped, knowing this was the moment. He'd wanted this for so long. He felt overwhelmed with lust, lightheaded with excitement. Jessie turned to look at him, an uncertain expression on her face. "It's up to her," he said looking into his wife's eyes.

Roman looked at Jessie, the question hanging in the air.

After a moment, and with a lopsided smile, she said "I guess I owe you that much. After passing out on you."

Roman smiled slightly. Then he leaned in and kissed her. He started slow, just soft kisses on her lips, then he placed his mouth fully on hers. He gently probed with his tongue, and she opened her mouth, and then his tongue was inside her mouth. They kissed for long minutes, and when they finally parted both were panting.

Still in Roman's arms, Jessie looked over at her husband. He had taken his cock out and was slowly stroking himself. "Sit down," she said turning back to Roman.

Jessie got on her knees between his legs and unbuckled and unzipped him. She pulled down his jeans and saw the huge tent in his shorts. Her hands practically shook as she pulled down his shorts.

Her eyes went wide. "Um ... really?" she said to herself in amazement as she gawked at the gigantic thing sticking up at her. It was huge, well over two hands long (maybe even three hands) and very thick, with big veins running up the sides and on the underside. She wrapped both hands around him. It was hard like granite, but the skin soft like a baby's skin.

Jessie looked again at her husband. He was still stroking his cock. She looked into his eyes and softly asked, "Are you sure?"

Ollie nodded. His face was a picture of unbridled lust. He wasn't looking at Jessie's face. He was looking at his wife's hands wrapped around Roman's cock.

Jessie looked back at Roman's cock. Then she opened her lips and took him into her mouth.

Roman moaned as he felt Jessie's soft lips envelope him. He could tell she wasn't used to his size, but she was doing a good job, better than good. He'd never had any girl so beautiful go down on him, and it made it even more exciting.

Roman wanted to wrap his hands around her head and thrust into her mouth, but he held back not wanting to hurt her. He'd done that to other girls, roughly fucked their faces. He'd done that to Alicia, and to the many girls he'd bedded since they separated. But he didn't want to do that to Jessie, she was too special. But he couldn't resist touching her, so he reached down and fondled her breasts.

Jessie could barely take any of Roman's cock in her mouth. He was just too thick. She loved the smell of him, the musty man smell. She felt his hands on her breasts and it felt good. She wanted to feel his hands on her bare skin. She released Roman's cock and took off her turtleneck.

Then she pulled off the hair tie and shook out her long blonde hair. She reached behind her and unsnapped her bra. She looked over at her husband. His pants and shorts were around his ankles. Crazed lust filled his face and he panted excitedly. His hand was wrapped around his penis. She noticed his hand almost completely engulfed his penis, only part of his cockhead extended past his hand. She'd known Roman was bigger than her husband, but until now it had been an abstract thought. Now though, their immense size difference became real to her.

Jessie took off her bra and let it drop to the floor. She turned back to Roman, seeing him stare at her chest. She waited for him to say something. When he didn't, she said timidly, "I guess not as big as Bianca's, huh? Or Alicia's?"

Roman finally tore his eyes from Jessie's tits and looked into her blue eyes. "They're beautiful," he said almost reverently, reaching with both hands and cupping her.

She smiled bashfully, blushing from Roman's compliment. She wrapped her hands around his rod and again took him into her mouth.

Roman gasped at the sensation of his cock once again in Jessie's soft mouth. His instinct was to roll his head back, but he couldn't tear his eyes from Jessie's beautiful face, her mouth open wide around his shaft. As her head moved up and down, her long soft hair fell onto his thighs. He gripped the armrests, as the sensations of her soft blonde hair swaying across his thighs as she bobbed her head up and down were incredible. He'd always been partial to girls with short hair, but now he realized what he'd been missing all his adult life.

"I'm gonna cum!" he groaned suddenly. He assumed she'd pull off and finish him with her hands – most girls (including Alicia) did that—but instead she swallowed more of his shaft. "Ugh, god!" he cried, and then he came, his hips bucking with every ejaculation, his hands instinctively gripping the back of Jessie's head and shoving more of his thick rod down her throat.

Jessie wasn't prepared for the amount of cum shooting out of Roman's cock. She thought she was going to gag. Then she felt his hands gripping her head and he shoved more of his cock down her throat. Tears rolled down her face. But somehow she held on and her throat muscles worked hard to swallow his cum, although some leaked from her mouth and ran down her chin. Finally she felt him softening in her mouth. When she finally let him drop from her mouth, all she could say was, "Wow. You cum a lot."

She wiped her mouth and chin with her hands, and then she wiped her wet hands on her jeans. She rubbed the tears from her cheek. She looked back at Ollie. He had cum too, his sperm on his hands. She went over to him and knelt at his feet. She softly stroked his cheek with her soft hand. "Are you okay?" she asked.

"Yes," he answered, but she saw hurt and uncertainty in his eyes.

"It's okay," she said softly, taking Ollie's hand and lovingly licking his cum from his fingers.

Ollie had felt jealous watching his wife go down on Roman, especially since she was so clearly enthralled by his cock. Ollie had known it was big, but he'd never imagined it would be that long and thick. It made him feel insecure but excited him at the same time. Even though he'd just cum his lust still overwhelmed him.

"Lay down," he said. He got on the floor and pulled off his wife's jeans, leaving her in just her black tights. He felt her crotch. She was soaking wet. He got between her legs and tore a hole in her pantyhose, exposing her glistening pussy. He went down on her. He heard her moan, and it made him feel good. He wanted to be the man who made her cum. At least for the first time tonight.

Ollie heard Jessie moaned again, and he licked harder, knowing how she liked it. But he felt her body writhe and twist, and sensed her moans weren't because of what he was doing. He looked up. To his surprise, Roman was kissing Jessie. He was fondling her breasts, rubbing her nipples between his thumbs and fingers, and she was stroking his cock which was already hardening again.

Jessie continued moaning even though Ollie was no longer eating her, so he knew for sure that it was Roman she was responding to, not him. In fact, he got the feeling Jessie hadn't even been aware of what he'd been doing. Roman's lips left Jessie's and he took her nipple into his mouth. Her body writhed as he licked and sucked her nipple, and then Roman's hand moved over her flat stomach and cupped her pussy.

With annoyance, Ollie wondered what Roman would've done if he'd still been eating her, push him out of the way? Jessie moaned and arched her back as Roman pressed his thumb against her clit. Ollie rose from between his wife's legs and sat back into the chair, feeling like a third wheel. Roman immediately got between Jessie's legs. Ollie knew he was about to see Jessie fucked. His wife was about to be fucked by another man.

This was what he wanted, right? What he'd fantasized about for years. But his heart felt about to break. He wanted to shout STOP! He wanted to pull Roman away from his wife and kick him out of their home. But he knew he couldn't do that again to Jessie. So he sat there dumbly, feeling as if in shock, like watching a train wreck about to happen.

Roman grabbed his big dick and aimed it at the opening Ollie had ripped in Jessie's pantyhose. He pressed it between her slim pussy lips and then leaned down on her. Jessie groaned and spread her long legs wider as the big head of his cock penetrated her.

Ollie would remember this moment for the rest of his life. The moment his wife's pussy was penetrated by another man's cock.

"Oh god you're big!" Jessie grunted, her eyes clenched shut.

"It's alright, just relax, I'll go slow," Roman said soothingly. He gently pushed against her over and over, slowly pushing in and then out, each time pushing a little more of his cock into her. Jessie grunted and her nostrils flared with each of his thrusts. She couldn't believe the incredible sensations of having something so big pushing into her, and how wonderful it felt. She'd had sex with other men before marrying, and most had been bigger than Ollie. But nothing like Roman. This was a totally new and unbelievable experience.

Roman took his time, patient and gentle, supporting himself on his muscular arms. Clearly he'd done this many times before, knowing how to indoctrinate a girl with his big cock for the first time. Finally with one of his thrusts he stayed in a push up position above her. He had enough of his cock inside so he could simply apply constant pressure until Jessie's pussy relaxed and gave way and that's exactly what happened as he expertly pushed himself into Jessie's pussy.

"Oh fuck!" Jessie grunted. "God you're so big!"

"Are you okay?" he asked gently kissing her lips.

"Yeah, yeah, just give me a minute to get used to it," Jessie panted.

Roman nodded. He was patient. He knew it took time for girls to get used to his size. He leaned down and kissed Jessie, making out with her as she got used to his big cock inside her. Jessie kissed him back, wrapping her arms around his neck and slipping her tongue into his mouth.

After long moments of kissing, Roman lifted himself up off of her, and then pushed back down, impaling her with his long thick cock. He did it over and over, Jessie's nostrils flaring each time he plunged into her, but she was becoming accustomed to his size. Sensing this, Roman lifted Jessie's legs (still in black pantyhose) onto his shoulders, and started fucking her harder and faster. It wasn't long before Ollie heard their bodies slapping together. Despite his mixed feelings, he was hard again and began stroking himself.

"Oh god oh god oh god," Jessie cried, her voice beginning to breakdown, no longer able to speak clearly. Her cries rose over the rapid slapping noise and Roman's own grunts. Roman's penis size and his sexual prowess were taking her to a new sexual level. Jessie whimpered as Roman continued his assault on her body, and then she began to sob ecstatically. It was obvious Jessie was experiencing something she'd never before had with any man, including her husband.

Roman kept up this brutal pace for an extraordinary length of time. Then Roman lifted Jessie onto the sofa. Ollie saw Roman was going to have even more leverage with his feet on the floor and God only knew what he was going to put his wife through now. He found out immediately as Roman began rapidly humping between Jessie' s legs. He could clearly see his enormous shaft slicing into his wife like a battering ram. It looked like a thick pipe made from shiny marble as it glistened with their combined excitement. Her moans and sobs of ecstasy were continuous, and her small stockinged feet flailed helplessly in the air with each of Roman's thrusts.

Ollie saw Jessie's body tense up and her feet arched. He knew she was about to cum.

"Ah ah ah ah!" was all Jessie could say as a huge orgasm built inside her.

Roman also knew she was about to cum. He said "That's it Jessie, let it happen, cum on my cock!"

"Oh Roman, oh fuck, fuck!" Jessie cried as her orgasm hit. Her body shuddered from the thunderous orgasm that rocked her body. Roman released her legs from his shoulders and leaned down, planting his lips over hers and kissing her through her orgasm. Ollie's jealousy peaked at the intense intimacy of the gesture, yet his body betrayed him and he lurched and once again ejaculated over his hand.

As Jessie writhed underneath him, Roman kept up a relentless rhythm. His endurance was incredible. To Ollie's dismay, her orgasm seemed to go on forever. Still kissing him, Jessie wrapped her arms and long legs around Roman, hugging him so close it was like they were a single person. Finally Roman slowed his pace, sensing Jessie's orgasm subsiding. He moved her to lie on the sofa, but they remained in their intimate embrace. He kept fucking her but slowed so he could whisper softly into her ear. They held each other and kissed as they whispered. Ollie could hear the whispers but couldn't make out what was being said. Occasionally Jessie would smile and nod her head at Roman, then they'd kiss some more.

With horror Ollie remembered Jessie had gone off the pill months ago, and she hadn't made Roman wear a condom. He knew Jessie had the condoms he gave her in her purse, but the idea of Roman coming inside her unprotected pussy made him lightheaded with wicked lust. For long moments, he was frozen with indecision.

Roman continued to fuck Jessie with slow, long strokes. Suddenly he moaned and his muscular back arched. Roman pumped hard into Jessie as he came.

With each orgasmic thrust, Roman ejaculated into Jessie, and each ejaculation was a powerful flood of his sperm into Jessie. She felt his cum blast against her vaginal walls and her eyes went wide. She had never experienced such sensations.

Afterwards, like before, they kissed and whispered softly to each other, with Jessie's arms around his neck, tenderly playing with his hair. Roman was still inside her but his cock softened, and Ollie's insides exploded as he saw thick milky cream leak from her pussy and coat her black pantyhose.

Jessie untangled herself from Roman. She stood up from the sofa and walked over to where her husband sat. Taking his hand, she walked him to their bedroom. Roman was gracious enough not to follow, to give them privacy.

Jessie finished undressing Ollie, then laid him onto his back on their bed. She sensed he wanted her to keep the pantyhose on. She got on top of him and straddled his hips. Then, taking his cock in her hand (he was already hard again), she lowered herself onto him.

They made love, Jessie moving slowly up and down on Ollie's cock. She hugged and kissed him, and said "I love you" over and over. After

Ollie came, they snuggled for a long time, not saying anything. Then they both fell asleep.

CHAPTER 5

When they woke the next morning, Roman was gone. Ollie woke before Jessie.

Then Jessie opened her eyes. "Hey you," she said sleepily.

"Hi," Ollie said, his one syllable reply carrying the weight of all his emotions.

Jessie smiled weakly. "It got really intense last night."

"Yeah. Really intense."

Jessie tried to read her husband's face. Not able to, she snuggled close to him. After a few moments of silence, she asked, "Was it good for you? Everything you wanted?"

It was a fair question, given how much he'd talked about it over the years. And how much he'd pressured and cajoled her to play his games. He made a decision not to reveal how he was really feeling. "It was great!" he said forcing a smile and trying to sound enthusiastic. "You were amazing!"

Jessie looked relieved. "I was afraid there. I know I got out of control a little. Sometimes you didn't look too happy."

He shrugged, but kept the smile planted on his face. "You know, I've told you, sometimes I get jealous and angsty, but that just adds to the excitement." He forced a chuckle, trying to keep things upbeat. "You did get out of control there. I guess you really enjoyed yourself."

"Well – yeah," she said with a laugh. She was careful with what she said. They were both walking on eggshells. "I mean, Roman's a good lover, but it wasn't all him. There was just so much build up with everything. I think it could've been Donald Trump and I would've cum." Then after a moment, she laughed and said "Okay, maybe not."

They both laughed. Then they kissed. Then Ollie moved on top of Jessie. He was hard. She reached between their bodies and guided his penis into her.

"How do I feel?" Ollie asked as he moved in and out of his wife. "My cock. How does it feel?"

"You feel so good baby," Jessie assured him.

"He's way bigger than me."

"Yeah but ..."

"But what?"

"I mean, he was actually too big," Jessie said. "I'm not sure I could take that much every night."

"Okay," Ollie said doubtfully.

"So you're perfect for me," Jessie assured him, kissing her husband.

"Okay," Ollie said again.

"You don't believe me?"

Ollie shrugged. "You came really hard with him," he said. "You've never cum that hard with me."

"How do you know? You give me amazing orgasms."

"Just the way you acted," Ollie said. "And the sounds you made. You've never been that way with me."

Jessie was silent for a moment as Ollie continued to slowly move in and out of her. "I think, you know, he was new," she said cautiously. "New is always exciting. And it's what I told you. I was already so worked up from all the playing at bars and that swinger club. So that's all it was."

"Okay," Ollie said, leaning down to kiss her. "I just want you to tell me the truth. I won't ask if I don't want to know."

"I will," Jessie said.

"So it was good? You had fun?"

"Well, yeah, I did," Jessie replied.

"Do you want to do it again?"

"You mean with Roman?"

"It could be someone else. It doesn't have to be Roman."

"I don't know," Jessie said hesitantly. "This game, it's exciting, but it makes me feel like a slut too sometimes. I wouldn't feel that way so much if it's Roman."

"Oh," Ollie said, his insides suddenly feeling queasy.

She saw it on his face and quickly added, "It's not because Roman's special or anything. He's not special to me. It's just, I know him, we're friends. If we do this with a friend, it's easier for me. Does that make sense?"

Ollie still felt queasy inside, and his jealousy was spiking, but it also got him hot that she wanted to be with Roman again. Moreso than if she fucked a series of random strangers. He grinned and joked, "And it doesn't hurt that he's got a big cock."

"Well yeah, there's that," Jessie joked back, and they both laughed.

———◉———

After their sex, they lay side by side, both of them panting, looking at each other. Ollie thought about how to say the next thing. He had to be careful. He didn't want Jessie to think he was putting this on her. She had a short temper and he didn't want her to get angry or defensive. He said carefully, "You know, we didn't make Roman wear a condom last night ..."

"Yeah, and he came so much," she said with a laugh. She remembered how it felt to feel his cum hitting her inner walls and she inwardly shivered. But then she realized the implications. "Oh my god ... I wasn't thinking ..."

Ollie quickly took her hands. "It's all my fault," he said. "I got caught up in the moment. I wasn't thinking either. But, I think we need to get you a morning after pill."

Jessie's lips parted in a small O. "Yes, I think you're right," she said softly. She'd gone off the pill a few months ago, as she and Ollie wanted to start a family. They were both still young, so at the moment, they weren't trying too hard to get pregnant, like monitoring her cycles. That would come later, if need be. For now, they were letting nature take its course.

So at the moment, she was completely unprotected. And Roman had cum inside her. He was clearly a very fertile man, having gotten Alicia pregnant 3 times.

Jessie thought about where she was in her cycle. She didn't know. She hadn't been tracking it. She hadn't expected this to happen.

Later that day, Ollie took Jessie to see her doctor, Irene. Morning after pills were over the counter, but she'd never taken one and didn't really know much about them. Jessie wanted to see her doctor to make sure there wouldn't be any side effects, especially with her ability to have children later.

"Well, that wasn't fun," Jessie said sourly as she emerged from the doctor's office and into the waiting room. "Irene knows we're trying to have a baby. So when I asked about the morning after pill, she asked me if I'm having an affair."

Ollie felt bad for her embarrassment. Irene had been Jessie's gynecologist since she was a pre-teen. "I'm sorry honey."

She shrugged, not looking at Ollie. "Whatever," she said dismissively, giving Ollie the cold shoulder. She was mad because she felt he'd gotten her into this. She knew it was unfair, but she couldn't help how she felt.

They went to the Long's pharmacy next to their apartment for the pill, and she swallowed it with a glass of water.

CHAPTER 6

A few weeks later, Ollie and Jessie saw Roman at church. He was alone, so they assumed it was Alicia's weekend with the kids. Ollie steered Jessie to Roman's pew. He couldn't stop thinking about their evening together. He'd gotten jealous and bothered, but survived it. Strong emotions were sure to follow after watching your wife get her brains fucked out by another man. But that's a big part of what made it so exciting, and he wanted it to happen again.

Just before reciting the Lord's Prayer, Ollie whispered into Jessie's ear. "Do you want to go home with him?"

"Ollie, no," she whispered back. "We're at freaking church. It's too awkward."

"I can talk to him."

"Ollie ..."

After the service ended and they were walking out, Ollie looked questioning at his wife. She gave him a non-committal shrug. He gave her a mischievous grin and caught up with Roman while she waited.

"Roman, wait up," Ollie said catching up. He motioned Roman to an unoccupied corner of the church's foyer. It was the first time they'd spoken since that evening, and he could tell Roman was feeling awkward. He gave him a friendly smile to put him at ease. "Do you have plans today? Picking up the kids or anything?"

"No, Alicia has the kids until tomorrow morning."

Ollie lowered his voice even more, looking around to make sure no one was within earshot. "Interested in coming over?"

Roman looked surprised. "Are you serious? You're not upset about the other night?"

Ollie smiled. "No—I told you I'm into that."

Roman slowly nodded, as if coming to grips with Ollie's wild fantasies. "Are you sure Jessie wants to?"

Ollie grinned. "Yes, I'm sure." Both men looked over to where Jessie stood.

She blushed as they looked at her, looking down at her feet to avoid their eyes. She couldn't imagine a more awkward situation. Ollie annoyed her with his one-track mind. But to be honest, she'd thought about that night – and Roman—a lot. It'd been incredible, and she wouldn't mind trying it – and him—again.

Outside in the parking lot, Ollie held the door open for Jessie. "Do you want to follow us?" he asked Roman.

"You know, I actually have to be close to home. Alicia said she might drop the kids off early. I think she might have a date." More awkwardness followed. Alicia might have a date, but that was nothing compared to what they were doing.

Ollie spoke up with an easy solution. "Why don't you two go over to your place? Honey, I'll be at home. Just call me when you want to be picked up."

Roman and Jessie rode in silence, and the awkwardness continued when they got to his house. The tension was so thick you could cut it with a knife. "Want a drink?" Roman finally asked.

"I'd love one!" Jessie said immediately. They looked at each other, and then burst out laughing.

"Are you okay with Alicia dating?" Jessie asked as Roman handed her a vodka martini.

"I don't care. I think she's doing it to make me jealous."

"Are you jealous?"

"No," Roman said dismissively with an air of finality.

Jessie thought he was being callous, but didn't say anything more, thinking it wasn't her business. She sat down with her wine and crossed her legs. Roman sat next to her, his eyes going to her legs. "I have to admit something to you," he said tearing his eyes from her legs and looking at her face. "Remember that time you came over to watch football, and you wore those holey jeans? I kept looking at that hole the entire day." He blushed in embarrassment. "I've never met a girl who wears pantyhose under jeans. It's sexy."

Of course Jessie remembered. His confession made her blush. "I guess I got in the habit in college. Freshman year, my business class was all the way across campus from the dance studio. So sometimes after dance class all I had time for was to pull on jeans over my tights to get to class on time."

Roman smiled lustfully. "You look incredible in leotards."

"How would you know?" she asked. She took a dance class at Roman's gym, but didn't remember him ever seeing her in dancewear.

Still smiling, he said, "Sometimes I use the security cameras to watch your dance class."

Jessie's eyes went wide. "Oh my god, you're a stalker!"

He laughed, hearing the playfulness in her voice. "I am when it comes to you." They both laughed.

Jessie got on her knees on the sofa and leaned into him, his arms immediately going around her waist. "Well, maybe I'll have to come over sometime in my leotard and tights. Would you like that?"

"I'd love that," he said as he kissed her, his hands cupping her firm ass cheeks. He was treated to the feel of a garter strap.

Jessie smiled sensing his excitement. "Do you like what I'm wearing?" she asked as she felt his hands disappear under her dress and explore her lingerie. "I thought the day might end this way. Ollie's been talking about that other night a lot."

"He's different, that's for sure."

"You're being too nice," she said giggling. "I think perverted is the right word. Maybe obsessed."

"Well, whatever it's called, I'm happy I get to spend time with you," he said. He ran his fingers along the lacy stocking tops, her bare skin above, the straps of her garter belt. "You wore this for me?"

"I did," she said huskily, getting turned on by his caresses. "Just for you. Like I said, I hoped the day would end this way."

Roman's heart leaped. She'd been thinking about him, and even dressed special for him.

He kissed her, and rolled her onto her back, pulling her skirt up as he did. Jessie's hands went to his chest, pulling off his tie and then unbuttoning his shirt. As he reached around her and unzipped her dress, she reached to his pants. In moments they were both completely nude, except Jessie still had on her bra, garter belt, stockings and heels (she hadn't worn panties, again because she hoped the day would end his way). Neither needed any foreplay, they were too hungry for each other. Roman got between her legs and aimed his cock at her pussy. He was about to push into her when Jessie remembered.

"Wait, Roman," she said, pushing on his chest. "In my purse. A condom."

Roman hated condoms. "Come on. We didn't need that last time."

"I know, but we have to." She reached over into her purse and pulled out one of the packages Ollie had given her. "I don't want to either, but …"

It was true, too, Jessie didn't want to use a condom. Skin-to-skin always felt better of course. But it was more than that. The first time, Roman had cum so much inside her, and so hard, she'd felt his sperm hitting her walls. That had been a new experience for her, and to be honest, she wanted to feel that again. But obviously that was not an option now.

Jessie tore open the package with her teeth. She used both her hands to roll the condom onto Roman's cock. Even though the condom was extra-large – "Super XL Magnum"—she still had difficulty getting it around his girth, especially the big head. And despite being extra large, it reached barely halfway down his long shaft.

Roman pulled Jessie's thong panties to the side. He moaned as he pushed his cock into her. "God you feel so good. You're so fucking tight. You feel so much better than Alicia."

Jessie grimaced as Roman pushed his cock into her. He was so freaking big! It felt amazing though. She'd never had a man so big. She loved how his thickness stretched her. And she loved how his length made her feel so full.

But she felt uncomfortable when he compared her to Alicia. Partly because they were still married so technically, Roman was cheating on his wife. And it made her think about Ollie. Her husband was much smaller compared to Roman. She definitely felt the difference. But that thought made her feel like she was betraying her husband.

Like before, Roman fucked Jessie long and hard, and when she came her orgasm was incredibly intense and seemed to go on forever.

Roman managed to hold off until Jessie came, but then he felt on the edge of cumming. He'd always been able to last. He wasn't a quick shooter. But Jessie's pussy felt too good.

"Fuck you feel so good!" he moaned. "Your pussy's so tight! And it's so smooth! It feels like a tight silk glove around my cock!" A moment later he came.

After they both came and caught their breaths, Roman began pulling out. "Wait," Jessie said quickly. She reached between their bodies and wrapped her thumb and index finger around the bottom of the condom. Roman was so thick, the tips of her thumb and finger didn't touch, but it would have to do.

"Careful," she cautioned as he pulled out. "Go slow."

Roman managed to pull out without the condom rolling off. The bulbous reservoir at the tip was flooded with thick milky cream. "Wow, I can't believe how much you cum," Jessie said.

He laughed. "Alicia always called it my super power."

Jessie grinned at the joke.

"Are you hungry? I can order Chinese food," Roman said. He took off the condom, wrapped it in some tissues and tossed it into the trash.

"That sounds awesome," she said. She began to take off her stockings but he stopped her.

"Can you leave that on?" he asked with a grin.

"Everything?" Jessie asked. She still wore the bra, garter belt, stockings and ankle strap heels."

"Would you mind?" Roman asked. "Alicia was always a plain bra and panties girl. So seeing you like that, it's pretty amazing. Especially with your sexy body. You look like a Victoria's Secret model."

Jessie gave a laugh. But again, she didn't feel comfortable when he compared her to his wife. She had to admit though, she loved the compliment. She was tempted to ask "What kind of underwear does Bianca wear?" but she was afraid of the answer. He might say "when you're that young and have big tits, it doesn't matter what kind of underwear you wear." That's something she didn't want to hear.

"Do you have a robe or something ... I'm kind of cold," she asked.

"Yeah, sure," he said looking around. "Is this okay?" he asked, handing his button down shirt from church to her.

Jessie paused. It was normally a big thing to put on a man's shirt. It was a sign of being possessed – of ownership. As Ollie's wife, she should only wear his shirts, since she belonged to him. But then she thought that was stupid, given how intimate she'd already been with Roman.

"Sure," she said, taking the shirt. She put it on. He was such a big man, she felt tiny in it. The shirt smelt like him. Sandalwood. She liked the smell.

After eating they had sex again. Their sex was fantastic (once again her orgasm was intense and lasted forever). After their breathing finally returned to normal, Roman pulled out. He was careful, but as he pulled out the condom ripped leaving a large glob of his sperm in her womb. "Damn!" she said, alarmed seeing the ripped condom.

"I'm sorry, I tried to be careful."

"I know you did. It's not your fault," she said. But she felt panicked as she looked down and saw milky cream leaking from her pussy lips.

"I don't get it. You didn't mind last time," Roman said.

"I'm not on birth control," Jessie told him. "Ollie and I are trying to have a baby."

"Oh," Roman said. Her revelation took him aback—but in a good way. Despite just cumming, he began stiffening again.

Jessie saw his cock growing hard.

Roman looked embarrassed. "Sorry," he said sheepishly. "I guess it's just instinct. Procreation of the species or something."

"Oh my god," Jessie said with a laugh. She was still laughing as she took off her lingerie and heels and went into the bathroom. She got into the shower and cleaned up as best she could.

Roman stood in the door of the bathroom, watching her shower. "So I guess we got lucky last time?" he asked.

"I took a morning after pill," Jessie told him. She stepped out of the shower and began drying herself.

"I'm sorry you had to do that," Roman said, looking regretful. "I would've gone with you if you told me."

"It was just a pill," Jessie said with a shrug. "And anyways, Ollie was with me. He's my husband. It's his job to be with me."

"Yes, of course," Roman quickly agreed.

"I better get going," Jessie said as they moved back into the bedroom. "I'll call Ollie to pick me up."

"No need. I'll drive you home," Roman offered.

"You don't have to do that," Jessie said as she put her bra on and began stepping into her dress.

"Wait …," Roman began, stopping her from dressing. He pressed his body against hers. "Don't go yet. We can do it again." Already he was fully hard again.

Roman kissed Jessie, and she kissed back. He explored her body and she dropped the dress. His hard cock, so heavy and thick, felt huge against her stomach.

Jessie's nipples hardened, and she felt tingling in her pussy. Her body was responding to him. She couldn't remember the last time she'd had sex 3 times in a single day – if ever – but she wanted Roman again.

But she knew Ollie was waiting at home. "I've really got to go," she said, managing to pull away from him. "You said you'll drive me?" she asked as she began dressing again.

Roman nodded. He looked disappointed. "When can we see each other again?" he asked as he began dressing too.

Jessie hesitated. Then she said "I have to talk to Ollie."

CHAPTER 7

When she got home, Ollie reclaimed his wife. He didn't wear a condom of course.

After cumming, he rolled off. With a chuckle in his voice, he said, "We're having so much sex, maybe you'll get pregnant. That would be kind of ironic with what we're doing."

Jessie frowned, looking concerned. "Ollie baby, I need to tell you something," she said. She sat up in the bed and looked into the face of her husband. "I made Roman wear a condom. But it ripped and some of his sperm got in me. I took a shower to wash, and I think I'm safe, but ...."

Ollie looked away from Jessie.

Jessie saw his reaction and became alarmed. "It's not my fault. It's not Roman's fault either," she insisted defensively. "We were careful. I guess I should take another morning after pill."

Ollie turned back to his wife. "That's not what I'm thinking," he said. He kissed her. "It's okay."

"What are you thinking?"

"I'm thinking what we're doing is risky," Ollie said. "All of it is risky. You did all you could. It's not your fault – or Roman's – the condom ripped."

"You're not worried?"

"Of course I am. But I don't think we should run out and get a morning after pill whenever something like this happens. Maybe we should use different condoms. I think Durex makes extra strong ones."

"I don't know ....," Jessie said hesitantly. The condoms they were currently using were ultra thin to feel as natural as possible. "Thicker condoms don't feel as good. And ..."

"What?"

"I mean ...," Jessie began, her cheeks going red. "Roman said how good my pussy feels. He said I feel better than Alicia." With an embarrassed laugh, she added, "He said I feel like a tight silk glove. So ...."

Ollie was silent for long moments, processing what she just told him. He was silent so long that Jessie looked concerned and said, "Are you okay?"

Ollie forced a smile. The jealous and angsty queasiness was churning through him again. He finally said, "I get it. You don't want to take that away from him. You want to feel good for him."

"Ollie baby, it's not about him. I mean, it's not about Roman specifically. He doesn't mean anything to me," Jessie assured her husband with a squeeze of his arm. "If you want me to be in this lifestyle, I mean, it would be the same for whoever I'm with. You know?"

"Yeah, I get it," Ollie said, looking down. He noticed, of course, that she was putting this all on him. He was okay with that. If that's what she needed to deal with this emotionally, he was okay putting this on him.

Jessie looked at her husband, trying to read his feelings. Abruptly she said, "I should go back on the pill."

"You can't," Ollie said immediately. "Remember what Irene said?"

Irene was Jessie's gynecologist. Jessie had been on the pill continuously since a teenager. During that time, she'd had some adverse reactions – not serious but uncomfortable, like rashes, migraines and upset stomachs. This caused Irene to vary the dosage or change the pill manufacturer a number of times. For this reason, Irene had also recommended against getting an IUD.

When Jessie went off the pill, Irene encouraged her to stay off the pill for at least 6 months, maybe longer, to let her body reset. That had been a little over 2 months ago. It hadn't seemed like a big deal back then, since they were trying to have a baby. But now ....

"Then what should we do?" she asked.

"I think we should just be careful, like we're doing now," Ollie said. After a moment, he asked, "Do you want to see Roman again?"

Jessie looked down at her feet. "I mean ...," she hesitantly began. "I guess if we keep doing this, then I'd like it to be with Roman. I know him, we're friends, and it's easier for me to do this with a friend. And it's like he's my secret lover. It's exciting, you know? It makes me feel like I'm in college again, doing crazy things. I guess I've missed that."

Ollie nodded slowly. Her desire to see Roman again made him jealous and excited at the same time. He knew it was risky for his wife to focus on just one man instead of a series of meaningless hookups. Strangely, that risk both increased his jealousy and excitement.

CONTINUED IN
OPENING PANDORA'S BOX
BOOK 3
JESSIE GROWS CLOSER TO ROMAN

Available at Amazon Kindle and Smashwords.

SNEAK PEEK – GIRLS WHO BELONG TO OTHER MEN BOOK 1

It started my first semester in college. I ran into Suzanne, a girl I knew from home. We ran in the same social circles in high school, but never interacted that much. She was always with Fred, her long-term boyfriend. But it was nice seeing a friendly face, so we went out for a beer.

One beer led to another, and pretty soon we were both feeling no pain. I walked her home. It started pouring as we reached her dorm, so she invited me in. Her roommate was away for the weekend visiting her boyfriend. We laughed drinking beer in her dorm room as the rain turned into a thunderstorm.

I'd never been interested in Suzanne. Not that she was a dog or anything. In fact she was pretty, with brown hair and a very cute, sweet face. She had big tits. Fred always raved about them whenever the guys got together. She was a little chubby though (I guess she'd be called pleasantly plump). Her legs were decent but not great.

I've always been more into skinny girls with long hair and great legs. So I never really thought much about her in high school.

And to be fair, she never gave me the time of day either. Like I said, she was committed to Fred. All through high school, they talked about getting married after college, and I figured that was still their plan.

But here we were together with it pouring outside. With my brain fogged by beer, Suzanne started to look good. On top of that, I think we were both homesick and lonely. So around midnight, with the rain still pounding against the window, I leaned over and kissed her.

She resisted at first, but I persisted, having gone an entire week without pussy. I thrust my tongue into her mouth, and eventually she began returning my kisses. I brought my hand between us and felt her tits. Shit they were big. I massaged her breast meat and rubbed her nipples. When she started moaning, I knew she wouldn't stop me unbuttoning her blouse.

She wore a plain tan bra with a front clasp. I opened it and gazed at her bare breasts. I'm not a tit man, but hers looked pretty good, shapely with just a little sag, and capped with enormous erect nipples. For a moment I envied Fred. Having these to play with all the time? Not the worst thing in the world.

I caressed Suzanne's soft flesh of her left breast, and leaned down and sucked her right nipple. She responded, moaning and arching her back. Pretty soon I had her writhing under me.

I moved my hands down to her jeans. As I began tugging them off, Suzanne put her hands on mine, stopping me. "I can't," she said between gasps. "I love Fred."

I knew it was a dick move. Suzanne was Fred's girl, and Fred was my buddy. But at that point, I was too horny to stop.

I kissed Suzanne and fondled her tits. I kissed her neck, caressed her breasts, thumbed her nipples, ran my hands down her back. I used all the tricks in my bag to get her super-hot so she would forget about Fred, at least until I got my dick inside her.

With one of her nipples in my mouth – her nipples were super sensitive, I could tell—I pulled down her jeans. This time she didn't stop me.

There was a wet spot in her panties. I fingered her and she groaned.

I curled my fingers into her panties and began pulling them down her fleshy thighs.

"Please don't," Suzanne pleaded.

"Fred never needs to know," I promised, kissing her again.

Suzanne kissed me back, and she even raised her ass when I began pulling down her panties again. I figured she was horny for cock. For years she'd probably been getting it regularly from Fred, but that had stopped when college started a few months ago. No sex for 3 months? I can barely last a week. No wonder she was horny.

When I pulled her panties off her feet – and I had to admit, while her legs were on the thick side, she had pretty feet – I took a moment to look at her pussy.

I was surprised to see her completely shaved. Like, full Brazilian. I had always thought of Suzanne as the bohemian-type, an oaks and granola kind of girl. So I expected a full bush. Seeing her bare like that made me realize how much effort she took to keep herself looking nice for Fred. As I looked at her shaved pussy, I thought to myself, "Fred buddy, lucky you, I think you found a winner with Suzanne."

Thinking about Fred didn't mean I wasn't going to fuck his girlfriend. Call me a dick, but the longer this night went along, the more I wanted to sink my man-meat into this chick.

I quickly pulled off my shirt and then tugged down my jeans and shorts. Suzanne's eyes were locked on my cock. I'd seen Fred naked in the gym shower after PE, and I knew I was bigger than him.

I reached into my wallet and pulled out the condom I always kept there. Suzanne watched as I ripped open the package and rolled the latex down my shaft. Her cheeks were flushed, and her eyes were heavy lidded. I could tell this girl was dying to be fucked.

I rubbed my cockhead up and down her slit. Her pussy lips glistened with moisture. As I began pressing into her, she put a palm on my chest to stop me.

"Go slow," Suzanne said.

"I will," I promised. As I got ready to thrust into her, she pushed against me with her palm again.

"You swear you'll never tell Fred?" she asked.

"I swear," I said, leaning down and kissing her. We kissed for a few moments, trading spit as our tongues danced together. Then, with her arms around my neck as we kissed, I pushed my cock into her.

Suzanne gasped as my cock penetrated her. "God ...," she groaned as I pushed deeper into her.

I went slow, taking my time, letting her get used to my length and girth. Finally when I was balls deep, we took a moment. We were looking at each other, panting into each other's face.

"Are you okay?" I asked her.

"Yeah, it's just ...," she said, panting. "You're really big."

"I'll be gentle," I said as I began moving in and out. As I began fucking Fred's girlfriend.

As Suzanne got used to my size, she began rocking back and forth with me, getting in sync with my thrusts. I squeezed her big tits and pinched her nipples as I fucked her, making her moan and roll her head back.

We were both getting close to the promised land when Suzanne's phone began ringing. "Oh god no!" she cried seeing the caller ID. "It's Fred!"

"Don't answer," I told her.

"I can't," Suzanne said looking panicked. "We always talk before going to sleep. If I don't answer he'll think something's wrong."

"Pull out," she said, pushing against my chest.

"I'm not pulling out," I told her. I was *not* going to end this night with blue balls.

Suzanne stared at me for long moments. Realizing I was serious, she urgently pleaded "Don't say anything, okay? And stop moving."

When I nodded, Suzanne put the phone to her ear. "Hi baby, um, I miss you so much, what'd you do today?"

I listened as they spoke, supporting myself on my arms. I thought I might grow soft as they spoke, but the wickedness of my cock buried deep inside Suzanne as she talked to Fred was keeping me hard.

I leaned down and nibbled on her neck. She pushed me away and glared at me. I leaned down again and kissed her lips even as she spoke to Fred. As I did, I heard Fred telling her about binging *The Last of Us*.

Suzanne pushed me away again. I reached down and squeezed her big tits. When I rubbed the flats of my thumbs over her nipples, she clenched her teeth to prevent herself from moaning.

"You should watch it," I heard Fred say. "It's as good as *The Walking Dead*."

"I will," Suzanne said with a strained voice. She was frantically shaking her head, trying to get me to stop. I ignored her and continued fondling her breasts. She squeezed her eyes shut, doing all she could to keep from moaning.

It excited me to hear Suzanne trying to carry on a normal conversation with her boyfriend with my cock buried deep inside her. I couldn't resist rocking back and forth. Suzanne's eyes went wide and again she frantically shook her head no.

Again, I ignore her. I slowly thrusted in and out. I was gentle, not pushing deep or hard. And I was quiet. Fred couldn't hear a thing (except maybe Suzanne's heavy breathing). But I was fucking her. While she was on the phone with her boyfriend.

Suzanne tried to talk normally to Fred, but I could tell the fucking was getting to her. I started taking slightly faster, slightly longer strokes, making her face flush with pleasure. Then I reached down and flicked my finger over her clit. This time she couldn't help moaning. Fred heard it.

"What was that, are you okay?" I heard Fred ask.

"Yeah, yeah, I'm okay, I'm just, ah, I'm just a little tired," Suzanne answered. She was panting.

"I really miss you Suzy," Fred said. "This long distance romance thing sucks."

"Yeah," Suzanne said. She was looking in my eyes as I continued to fuck her. She had a desperate, frantic look on her cute chubby face.

"I can't wait until Christmas break," Fred said. "I can't wait to see you."

Suzanne pressed both her hands on my chest. Her eyes begged me to stop.

I decided to be nice. I stopped fucking her, but I didn't pull out.

"I can't wait to see you too," Suzanne said to Fred. She was still breathing hard, but at least now she wasn't getting fucked as she said lovey things to her boyfriend.

"I love you Suzy," Fred said. There was so much emotion in his voice. I heard it, and so did Suzanne. It got me hot that he was professing his love for his girlfriend while she was impaled on my hard cock.

Suzanne's eyes teared up. She was thinking the same thing as me. But while it got me hot, she felt sad and regretful since she was betraying the man she loved.

"I love you too Freddie," Suzanne said. "I guess I better get going. I have an early class tomorrow."

"Okay. Bye. I love you," Fred said.

"I love you too," Suzanne said. Then she pushed the button to end the call.

Suzanne looked into my face. Tears ran down her cheeks. But she didn't tell me to pull out, or try to push me away.

I leaned down and kissed her. She kissed me back, wrapping her arms around my neck.

I began moving in and out again. She gripped my arms as I began fucking her faster and harder.

I put Suzanne's legs on my shoulders, and began to really fuck her. I rammed her pussy hard and fast.

"Oh god, oh god, oh god, oh god ...," she moaned. Her moans were continuous now. I was pretty sure Freddie had never fucked her so hard. Or so good.

I felt Suzanne's pussy squeeze around my cock, and then she was thrashing about as she came. She clamped her hands over her mouth to muffle her screams so her dormmates wouldn't hear her cum.

I wanted to orgasm in Suzanne's pussy. But something came over me. For years in high school, I'd seen them kiss. Suzanne kissing Fred.

I wanted to cum in her mouth. I wanted her lips that kissed Fred all those years wet with my jizz.

So just as I was about to cum, I pulled out. I quickly pulled off the condom and then I moved up to her face. I pushed my cock into her mouth.

SNEAK PEAK – HUSBAND ENCOURAGES WIFE

C hapter 1
Alicia walked into her bedroom, her face still flushed from the conversation at lunch. Her pussy throbbed. She didn't normally masturbate in the middle of the day, but she needed relief, and the kids would be at the sitter's for a few more hours. She lay on the bed and pulled up her skirt. She touched herself. Her panties were so wet. She slipped her hand inside her panties and rubbed herself, her eyes closed, remembering what Tina had told her at lunch.

"Wow, what's this?" a surprised voice said from the doorway.

"Oh my god!" Alicia cried in embarrassment, pulling the covers over her. "Myles, what are you doing home so early?"

Myles laughed, enjoying his wife's embarrassment. "My meeting ended early, so I decided to come home. I'm glad I did." Myles threw the covers off his wife. Her dress was still bunched around her waist, and he admired her long shapely legs. Even after 10 years of marriage, he couldn't get over how fantastic her legs were.

"Stop!" she protested, trying to pull the covers back up, but Myles laughed again and batted her hands away. Alicia covered her blushing face with her hands. "I can't believe you caught me playing with myself."

"So, what got you so excited?" Myles said as he put his hand on his wife's knee. "Did you watch Dr. McDreamy on Grey's Anatomy?" he teased. But he suspected why his wife was so aroused in the middle of the day. "Or, did Tina tell you more about her sex life over lunch?"

"Oh my god, you won't believe what she did last night," Alicia said excitedly. Tina and Alicia had been best friends since high school.

Tina divorced about six months ago, after catching her husband Bill cheating on her. Not yet ready for a serious relationship, but craving male companionship, she started going out with younger men about 2 months ago. Still pretty and desirable at 34, Tina pleasantly discovered that she didn't lack for male attention, and soon she was sleeping with a new young stud every few days.

"She met a guy at a bar last night," Alicia said. "He was only 23, in grad school! She let him pick her up. He took her to his apartment, and his roommate was there. Both guys started flirting with her, and before she knew it all three were in bed! She ended up doing it with both of them!"

Myles pulled off his pants and climbed between his wife's legs. "Did Tina like getting gangbanged by those two college kids?"

Alicia moaned as her husband pushed into her. "She said it made her feel so slutty. She had one guy in her mouth, while the other was inside her. Then they traded places, and she felt so naughty tasting herself."

"Did they make her cum?" Myles grunted as he pumped his cock in and out of his wife's pussy.

"Yeah," Alicia gasped, her own orgasm near. "She said it was incredible. She'd cum with one guy, and then the other would take his place."

"Oh god!" Myles groaned as he came in his wife. Alicia came too, her toes curling and digging into the mattress.

"Wow," Myles sighed a few minutes later. "That was great."

Alicia giggled and poked her husband's side. "I bet you were thinking about Tina when you came," she teased. "You like hearing about how she's being so slutty. It turns you on. Come on, admit it."

"Okay, I admit it, Tina's attractive," Myles said honestly. "But you know what really turns me on? It's you, getting so excited hearing about Tina acting like a slut."

"What?" Alicia asked, surprised.

"I'm not kidding. I guess in my head, I'm thinking you're wishing it was you, not Tina, getting fucked by those guys."

Alicia's jaw dropped. "And that turns you on? Thinking about me with other guys?"

Myles laughed. "Come on, don't be such a prude. There are a lot of guys with that fantasy. They even have a name for it, it's called 'hot wife' fantasy."

Alicia glared at her husband. "I know what they call it, Myles, I don't live in a fishbowl. I just never thought my husband was one of those prevents who wanted to see his wife fuck other men."

"Hey, wait a minute," Myles said, holding out his hands. "You're the one beating off in the middle of the day."

"I don't want to talk about it anymore!" Alicia said, getting out of bed and pulling down her dress. "Come on, the kids will be home soon."

Chapter 2

"What do you think of Jason, isn't he gorgeous?" Tina asked excitedly. Myles and Alicia looked toward the restaurant door. Jason had gone outside for a smoke.

"Uh, yeah," Alicia said. She felt awkward talking about Tina's new boy-toy in front of Myles. "Where did you meet him?"

Tina shrugged. "At a bar—where else?"

Myles laughed. "It must have been a college bar. What is he, 19?"

"Twenty-four, you jerk!" Tina said, playfully punching Myles in the arm. "And it wasn't a college bar, it was a hotel downtown."

"Excuse me," Alicia said, standing up. "I have to go to the bathroom."

"I guess you don't approve of my new love life," Tina said to Myles as Alicia walked away.

"That's not true. I know Bill treated you like shit, and you've had a rough year. I'm happy to see you're happy again."

Tina broke into a big smile. "Thanks for being so understanding." She reached under the table and squeezed Myles's thigh. "It's such a relief to hear you say that. I've been worried my friends would think less of me."

"No, not at all," Myles said, his voice caught in his voice. Tina's hand on his thigh almost made him shudder with excitement. She was so different from Alicia. She was a pretty brunette with large breasts. Alicia, in contrast, was a petite blonde with CoverGirl good looks, with small perky breasts. Tina wasn't leggy like Alicia, but her legs weren't bad. Thinking about this, Myles's eyes wandered down to Tina's legs. Myles admired how, since her divorce, her skirts had gotten shorter and shorter. He also liked the way she wore fuck-me pumps with high stiletto heels.

Myles noticed that Tina's skirt had hiked up her legs. His eyes widened when he saw the lacy welt of her stockings. He realized she was wearing thigh highs! That surprised him; he didn't think girls wore them in real life. He thought things like that (real stockings and garter belts) were incredibly sexy, but Alicia never wore them, preferring pantyhose.

Tina followed Myles's eyes, and realized she was flashing her stocking tops. "Oops, sorry," she said, embarrassed. She pulled down her skirt. Tina shrugged. "Okay, I admit it, I'm a slut. But stockings are better than pantyhose—less fumbling and easier access."

"Uh, no problem," Myles managed to say, his throat dry. "Like I said, you're entitled."

Tina smiled, and again squeezed Myles's thigh. "Thanks!" Tina let her hand linger on Myles's thigh, only pulling away when Alicia approached the table.

Jason returned a few minutes later. As they ordered drinks and then studied the menu, Jason's hands were all over Tina. Tina giggled and pushed him away, but he was relentless, caressing her legs under the table. When the drinks arrived, he gulped down his beer, then stood up, pulling Tina up with him. "Come on, baby, let's get a smoke."

Giggling, Tina said "We'll be right back," then let Jason lead her outside.

Awkwardly, Myles and Alicia continued to study their menus. Then Myles reached under the table to Alicia's legs. "Don't," Alicia said as Myles moved his hand under her skirt. But Myles wouldn't stop, and Alicia gasped when he touched her pussy. She had soaked through her panties and pantyhose. Myles pulled his hand away when the waitress came to take their order. Myles told her their friends would be back in a few minutes, they went out for a smoke.

About 10 minutes later, Tina and Jason finally returned. They ordered, and then Jason got up.

"I need a smoke," he said.

Alicia frowned at Jason's disappearing form. "I thought you guys just had a smoke," she said, annoyed. Alicia looked at Tina, who had a mischievous smile on her face. "What?" Alicia asked.

Tina hesitated, debating with herself whether she should tell them or keep quiet. But she couldn't hold it in. "Oh my god," she said elatedly. "We just did it!"

Alicia's eyes grew wide. "You're kidding?"

"No!" Tina almost shouted, her face excited and covered with a big smile. "He pulled me into the alley next to the restaurant, and he did me against the wall! Oh my god, we were right around the corner, I could hear the people walking on the sidewalk!"

"Oh no," Tina said in a concerned voice.

"What's wrong?"

"I can feel him running out of me. I'll be right back, I have to go to the bathroom, I don't want the back of my dress to get wet."

When they got home from dinner, Myles paid the babysitter while Alicia checked on the kids. Then, by silent agreement, they met at their bedroom. They groped each other like teenagers, practically ripping off each other's clothes.

"Fuck me!" Alicia pleaded. Myles pulled off Alicia's pantyhose and panties, then pulled out his cock.

"You so wet!" Myles growled as he penetrated his wife. "Did it turn you on, Jason fucking Tina in the alley like a whore?"

"Did it turn you on?" Alicia answered as she pushed back against her husband's thrusts.

Myles's passion fueled words came out between pants. "It turned me on, imagining it was you instead of Tina. Imagining Jason was fucking you against the wall."

"Oh god, you're so bad," she moaned.

"I'd like to watch you act like Tina. Become a cougar. Let young guys pick you up, and go home with them and let them fuck you."

"Oh god, Myles," Alicia panted between moans. "You don't mean that. I'm your wife."

"I want you to be my hot wife," Myles said lustfully. "Didn't you see how muscular Jason was? Wouldn't you like to feel a young hard body on top of you? Ramming his big cock into you? Shooting gallons of his cum into you, so it floods out of you and runs down your legs?"

"Oh Myles, would you really want me to do that?" Alicia cried as she raised her hips to meet her husband's thrusts. They were both so close, their passions fueled by their nasty fantasies.

"Yeah, yeah, that's all I've been thinking about since Tina started slutting around! I've imagined you in her place, being a slut with all those young guys!"

"Oh god, oh god," Alicia cried as she came, Myles joining her just seconds after.

"You haven't touched your lunch," Tina said after she finished telling Alicia about her latest date with Jason.

"I'm sorry," Alicia said. "I guess I'm distracted."

Tina reached over and grabbed her friend's hand. "What's wrong? Are you and Myles okay?"

Alicia looked up in surprise. "How did you know?"

"Alicia, we've been friends since high school," Tina said, concern in her voice. "I was your maid of honor. I think I can tell when things aren't going right with you and your husband. So what's wrong?"

"It's just—god, this is so embarrassing. But I've told Myles some of the things you've told me. You know, about the dates you've had with younger guys. Lately, Myles's told me about some things he fantasizes about."

"Oh," Tina said, her interest suddenly more than just concern for her friend. Has Myles been fantasizing about sleeping with her? She remembered the dinner the other night, when she put her hand on Myles's thigh. She shouldn't have, but she couldn't resist. She could tell he was hard. It gave her a naughty thrill to flirt with her best friend's husband. It was something she'd never have done while she was married, but she had embraced her new-found freedom since her divorce, especially since she'd started going out with younger guys.

Alicia hesitated, considering whether to tell Tina. But then she realized she needed to tell someone, and who better but her best friend. "You can't tell Myles I told you this."

"I promise," Tina said immediately, trying to hide her intense curiosity.

"Myles told me that—he has fantasies about—about seeing me with other men."

"What?" Tina said, wide-eyed. "You and other men?"

"Yeah, I know, it's crazy. He's never mentioned it before. It's only been since you've been going out with younger guys. He even said he fantasized it was me who Jason did in the alley."

"Wow," Tina said, shocked. She had heard some guys had this fantasy, but Myles seemed so straight-laced. Also, she remembered when Alicia started dating Myles, over 10 years ago. Myles had been jealous of guys even speaking to Alicia. She couldn't believe Myles had changed so much, that now he'd like to watch Alicia in bed with another man. "Do you think he really wants you to do it?"

"I'm not sure," Alicia said. "I don't think so, but he always talks about it ... I mean, when we're in bed."

"Well—okay, I know you're going to think this is crazy," Tina began, "but maybe you should hope that Myles is serious."

Alicia frowned at her friend. "You're right, I think you're crazy."

"No, I'm not crazy," Tina said, laughing. "You wouldn't believe how great sex is with these guys. They're so young and strong and gorgeous, and so hard! I'm glad Bill cheated on me, and we divorced. I really am! Because now I'm having the greatest sex of my life. He's paying me alimony, and I'm using his money to get all dolled up for other men."

Alicia's frown deepened. "So how does this all relate to me?"

Tina squeezed Alicia's arm. "Honey, I'm saying you can have the best of both worlds. You can be married to a great guy who loves you, and fuck other guys on the side. You're the luckiest girl in the world!"

Alicia shook her head. "Breaking my marriage vows isn't something I want to do."

"Alicia, it's not cheating if Myles wants you to do it," Tina insisted.

"I don't know about that," Alicia said skeptically. "Besides, I don't know if Myles is really serious about this."

"What if he is serious? Would you play along?" Tina smiled affectionately at her friend. "I mean, it would be fun to have someone to go clubbing with, like we did back in college."

"I don't know," Alicia said honestly. "Those days were a lot of fun. But I've been married for over 10 years, and I have two children. I love Myles. I don't want to break my marriage vows."

"But Alicia, honey, Myles wants you to do this. You wouldn't be breaking your marriage vows."

Alicia shook her head. "I told you, I don't know if he really wants me to do this."

"Okay, I have an idea," Tina said. "Come clubbing with me Saturday night. Just you, not Myles. See what he says."

"I don't know," Alicia said warily.

"Alicia, what's the harm? This will help you and Myles figure out what he really wants. He probably doesn't know himself. And it's not like you have to let some guy pick you up. We can just go out and have fun, like we used to do in college."

Alicia thought about it for a few moments, then she found herself nodding.

"**C**an we talk?" Alicia asked. "I mean, we haven't really talked about the other night."

They were at dinner, at a downtown restaurant. Alicia didn't want to talk about this in bed, or even at home. She wanted Myles to be thinking with his head and heart, not his penis.

"Sure," Myles said, putting down his menu. "It probably seems like my fantasy came out of nowhere, but it didn't. I've had these fantasies a long time, I just never had the courage to tell you."

"Really, of watching me with other men?" Alicia said, surprised.

"Yeah. It's always excited me, watching guys flirt with you. Remember last year, at our vacation in Cancun, when that guy hit on you? He kept asking you to dance? My cock was so hard I thought I was going to burst through my pants."

"Wow," Alicia said, wide-eyed with surprise. "Why didn't you ever tell me about your fantasy?"

"I don't know," Myles said, looking sheepishly. "It's hard to tell your wife that you fantasize about other men fucking her. But I guess, well ... lately, whenever Tina told you about one of her dates, you got really excited. I've thought maybe you might be open to some games."

Alicia frowned. "What kind of games, Myles?"

"You know what I'm talking about," Myles said.

"No, Myles, I want you to say it, tell me exactly what you want."

"Okay," Myles said. He was getting excited, and so he was trying to control his breathing. "I'd like you to go on dates with younger guys, like Tina does."

"Just like Tina?" Alicia asked. She wanted to find out how far Myles wanted her to go. "You know that Tina lets them kiss her, right? You'd want me to let another man kiss me?"

"Yeah, I would," Myles said without any hesitation. "As long as that's what you wanted."

"What about touching me? Do you want me to let another man touch my breasts?"

"Yes," Myles said, almost gasping with excitement. "I'd want you to let him fondle you."

"What if he put his hand on my leg? Would you want me to let him do that? What if he ran his fingers under my skirt? Should I let him do that, too?"

"Yeah, god, I'd want you to let him do that," Myles gasped. "God, you've gotten me so excited."

Alicia shook her head. "I don't understand how this turns you on."

"I can't explain it, but it does." Myles looked around to make sure no one was looking. Then he took his wife's hand and lowered it to his crotch. "See?"

Alicia's eyes grew wide with surprise. Myles was rock hard. His excitement was starting to turn her on. Also, she couldn't deny the naughty allure of a young, hard body. She massaged him under the table. "Tina wants me to go out with her Saturday night."

"She does?" Myles asked. "I think you should go!"

"Why?" Alicia asked, acting coy. She continued to massage him. "Do you want me to play your game?"

"Oh god, yes!" Myles said excitedly. "I want you to flirt with other men. I want you to kiss them, and let them touch you. God, I want you to touch their cocks, and suck them, and even fuck them!"

Alicia's breathing was heavy now. She was soaking wet. "Come on," she said urgently. "Let's pay the check, and go home!"

Chapter 3

Alicia was going to be late. Tina was going to be there any minute, and Alicia still wasn't dressed. It had been a long time (over 10 years!) since she had gone out dancing without Myles, and she didn't know what to wear. She finally picked out a silk, white blouse and a black skirt that ended a couple of inches above her knees. Underneath, she wore a bra, panties and pantyhose. She finished the outfit with black pumps.

Tina had already arrived when Alicia finally came downstairs. She smiled when she saw her friend. "Wow, now I understand what husbands mean when they say it takes forever for their wives to get dressed," Tina teased.

"Sorry," Alicia said sheepishly, kissing her friend on the cheek. "I couldn't figure out what to wear."

Tina stepped back and looked at Alicia. "Hmmm," she said as she studied what Alicia was wearing. She motioned to her skirt. "Don't you have anything shorter?"

"No," Alicia said, feeling uncomfortable under Tina's scrutiny. She felt like a school girl being evaluated by the headmistress.

Tina frowned, but then shrugged. "That's okay. Anyway, this will help." Tina handed Alicia a shoe box. "I thought you might not have any going-out-dancing-shoes."

Alicia opened the box and pulled out a pair of black high heels. "Dancing shoes?" Alicia said, fingering the 3-inch stiletto heels."

"Don't worry, they'll be plenty of guys there to catch you if you fall," Tina said, giggling. Then she playfully jabbed Myles in the arm. "Right Myles?"

"Uh, right," Myles said. Waiting downstairs for Alicia to get dressed had been excruciating, but exciting too. All Myles could think about was his pretty wife in the arms of another man while dancing at the club. He was so hard it hurt.

"God, you have great legs, I hate you," Tina said admiringly as Alicia slipped on the high heels. "Doesn't she have great legs, Myles?"

Myles could only nod; his throat was dry from excitement. Alicia did have amazing legs. They were her best feature next to her pretty face. He had always encouraged his wife to wear higher heels, but she always tended towards the more practical, low heel pumps. Now wearing the 3-inch stiletto heels, Alicia's legs looked even more incredible. His penis throbbed in his pants.

"Oh, you have great legs too," Alicia said to Tina. Then she tentatively began walking across the room. "How are you supposed to walk in these things?" Alicia said exasperated as she wobbled in the high heels.

Tina giggled. "It just takes practice. Anyway, I told you, they'll be plenty of guys there to catch you if you fall." Tina smiled and then, after making sure Alicia wasn't looking, she teasingly ran a finger across Myles's back, just below his belt.

Myles tensed at Tina's touch, her finger sending an electric charge through his body. He had always been attracted to her, now more than ever. He wondered if Tina teased guys when she went clubbing. Of course she did, Myles thought. That's how she picks up so many young guys. Myles's cock pulsed as he imagined Tina teaching his wife all her tricks for teasing men.

Tina lowered her voice so only Myles could hear. "Anyway, when guys catch you, that's the fun part, right Myles?"

Myles reddened. What had Alicia told Tina? Did Tina know about his fantasy to see Alicia with another man? Myles felt embarrassed. Men were supposed to be kings of their castles. They weren't supposed to let other alpha males fuck their wives. Yet, that was Myles's fantasy, and now Tina knew it. Why had Alicia told her?

"I'll wait for you at the car," Tina said to Alicia. As she left, she glanced again at Myles, a smile on her face.

"Are you sure about this?" Alicia asked Myles. "It's not too late to change our plans. All three of us could go to dinner."

Myles looked at his wife. Her makeup was perfect, her shoulder-length blonde hair lush and soft. The stiletto heels seemed to turn her otherwise conservative outfit into something reeking of sexuality. He found her almost impossible to resist, and he was tempted to take her to bed. But he knew if she, his wife, had this effect on him, her allure to other men would be even greater. He was becoming obsessed by his fantasy of her with another man.

"Yes, I'm sure," he finally said, his voice almost quivering from excitement. His earlier brief anger had been completely replaced by his lust. "I'll be awake when you get home."

⸻ ◉ ⸻

"God, I can't believe I'm here," Alicia said. She and Tina were sitting at the bar, sipping Cosmopolitans.

Tina smiled and squeezed Alicia's arm. "Don't be nervous, we're going to have fun."

Alicia frowned. "I know, but ... I guess I'm disappointed. I hoped Myles would change his mind. Playing this game of his isn't exactly what I imagined when we took our marriage vows."

"Alicia, you guys are just going through a phase, that's all. Who knows what happens to guys as they get older. At least Myles isn't trying to sleep with other women. I think you need to play this out, so Myles can get it out of his system."

"Yeah, I guess you're right," Alicia said after a few moments. "I just don't know how far he wants me to go. Or maybe I do know, but I'm not willing to go that far."

"So don't worry about it. Just take one step at a time, and let things go where they go." Tina hopped off the stool and grabbed Alicia's hand. "Come on, let's dance!"

Tina led Alicia into the middle of the dance floor. It was crowded, so they danced close together. Alicia was having fun, she hadn't been out dancing in years. The music changed to a slow song, and Alicia was about to go back to the bar when Tina grabbed her hand. She leaned close to Alicia's ear and whispered, "Some cute guys are watching us. No, don't turn! Just follow my lead."

Tina moved close to Alicia and danced slow. As she swayed, her fingers grazed across Alicia's skirt. At times she whispered into Alicia's ear, and as she did she allowed her fingers to trail down Alicia's back. She edged even closer to Alicia, until their breasts almost touched. Tina put her hands on her friend's waist, and they swayed to the soft music as one, Tina's fingers lightly caressing just above Alicia's ass.

Alicia knew what Tina was doing, of course. They had done this back in college, a little dirty dancing to get guys' attention. But that had been long ago, and Alicia wasn't used to the singles scene. She felt uncomfortable, but she played along with her friend (although she didn't touch Tina, the way Tina was touching her). She had to admit, though, that acting so sexy and drawing so much male attention was starting to turn her on.

Alicia was relieved when the song ended. Not waiting for Tina, she made her way back to the bar. She didn't want to give Tina a chance to dance another song. When Alicia looked back, she saw Tina surrounded by guys. They all looked well under 25.

Most of the guys were in suits. Alicia guessed they were attorneys just out of law school, or maybe Wall Street brokers. They were cute, but nothing special. Alicia was about to take a sip of her Cosmo when she saw him. He was tall, with thick wavy black hair, slicked back off his face. He had a dark complexion. Alicia guessed he was Greek or Italian. He was ruggedly handsome, and had a bad boy swagger to him. He wore a black turtleneck, jeans and boots. With a start, Alicia realized she was staring at him, and was about to turn away, when he turned towards her and locked eyes with her. His gaze was so intense it startled her, and she almost dropped her drink. Embarrassed, Alicia expected he would laugh at her, but he didn't. He just kept staring at her from across the room. After a few moments, Alicia turned away, but it took a force of will to escape from his intense gaze. Alicia found herself almost trembling, and she realized she was aroused. She finished the Cosmo and ordered another one.

A few minutes later Tina came back. "Come on, let's dance!" Tina said, dragging Alicia off the stool.

"Wait," Alicia said, and she quickly gulped down the martini. Then she let Tina drag her back onto the dance floor.

The martinis were working their way through Alicia's body, and helping her to lose her inhibitions. She was having fun, so when the music slowed, she didn't object when Tina moved closer for another round of dirty dancing. "We got those guys so hot the last time!" Tina whispered gleefully into Alicia's ear as they danced. "I thought they were going to drag me into a booth and rape me!"

As they danced, Tina reached lower so her fingertips trailed up Alicia's legs. She didn't stop when she reached Alicia's skirt, instead tracing up her thighs and bringing Alicia's skirt up as she did so. Alicia wondered if Tall-Dark-and-Handsome was watching her, and that thought combined with the two Cosmos made her more daring. As they danced close, Alicia lightly ran her fingers down Tina's back (she soon discovered Tina wasn't wearing a bra), then along Tina's hips. Their faces were so close their lips were almost touching. As they slowly swayed back and forth, sometimes Alicia's breasts would brush against Tina's.

The song ended, and as Alicia and Tina stepped apart, the crowd applauded. Tina smiled and did a curtsy, but Alicia was embarrassed and blushed. She quickly went back to the bar and ordered another Cosmo.

Alicia looked back and saw that Tina had disappeared. Some of the guys were gone as well. Alicia wondered if she'd see Tina again that evening.

Alicia ordered a Cosmo, and was searching in her purse for her wallet when she heard a deep, husky voice behind her.

"I'll get that," the voice said, and Alicia turned to see Tall-Dark-and-Handsome giving the bartender a twenty.

Alicia's heart did a back flip as she looked into his dark eyes. "Oh, that's not necessary," she stammered out.

"I insist. I'm Darius," he said, holding out his hand.

"Hi," Alicia said, taking his hand. Darius's hand was so large, Alicia's hand disappeared within his. For some reason, it didn't surprise her that his hand was rough and calloused. "I'm, ah, I'm Alicia. Darius—that's an unusual name."

"Yeah, it's Greek." I was right, Alicia thought. He's Greek.

Darius made no move to release Alicia's hand. Alicia began feeling uncomfortable so she pulled her hand back. Darius didn't stop her, but he extended his fingers so his fingertips traced along her soft palm as she pulled her hand away. The feeling almost made Alicia shudder. To hide it, she quickly took a drink of her Cosmo.

"You're a great dancer," Darius said.

Alicia blushed again. "I guess it got a little bit out of control."

Darius smiled. "Well, you looked great out there. You should lose control more often."

Alicia laughed. "Thanks ... I guess." Then they both laughed.

"So, do you come here often?" Alicia asked, but then she immediately put her head in her hands in embarrassment. "Oh god, I'm sorry, that's such a cliché." Why was she so nervous, she was acting like an idiot.

"That's okay," Darius said, laughing. "Yeah, my friends and I come here every couple of weeks. It has a reputation for being a meat market, but we like the music."

Alicia eyed Darius skeptically. "Soooooo, you're not here to pick up girls?"

Darius smiled mischievously. "That all depends on the girl. Like you, for instance."

"Not so fast, cowboy," Alicia said, laughing and shaking her head. She couldn't believe how forward this guy was, but she guessed that's how it was nowadays. "First of all, I'm way older than you. What are you, 24?"

"Twenty-five," Darius corrected. "And I prefer older women. I told you how good you look. You're the best looking girl in here."

"Yeah, well, whatever," Alicia said with a dismissive brush of her hand, but inside she was beaming from the compliment. "Second, I'm a married girl." Alicia held up her left hand, showing him her wedding ring. "See?"

Darius frowned. Then, looking serious, he waved his hand around the world. "Look around here, Alicia. Most of the girls are married. And I can tell you, the guys they're with aren't their husbands. This is how things are now. 9-11 could happen again tomorrow, or next week. We're all living on borrowed time. Life is too short to be limited by old-fashioned boundaries like marriage. We all need to embrace every second of our lives."

Alicia eyed Darius. Then she frowned. Then she started to laugh. "Oh my god, that has got to be the worst pick-up line I've ever heard!"

Darius started to laugh too. "Hey, I worked hard to come up with that!"

"Well, I think you better go back and start all over," Alicia said, still laughing. "And it's horrible to use 9-11 to try to pick up girls."

Darius held up his hands in mock surrender. "Okay, okay, you win, I have been properly chastised." Then he offered his hand to her. "So, do married girls dance?"

Alicia considered for a moment. Tina was no where to be found. And Darius seemed nice enough. She took his hand, making a snap decision. "Sure, why not?"

Darius was a good dancer. His movements were slow and smooth, yet perfectly paced with the music. Alicia couldn't believe a man as big as him could dance so well. He was well over 6 feet, and broad shouldered. She felt tiny next to him. As he moved to the music, Alicia could see the muscles of his chest and arms rippling under his black turtleneck. His broad shoulders narrowed to a lean waist, and from what Alicia could tell, Darius filled out his jeans really well.

Darius danced close to her, with barely any space between them. But he never touched her, never even brushed against her. Somehow, this close but non-contact, for song after song, was more of a turn on than if he was grinding his body against hers. She could feel herself get wet between her legs.

Eventually, the fast songs changed into a slow song. She expected Darius to pull her into an embrace, but he didn't. Instead, he stood there, so close to her but not touching her, looking at her with his intense black eyes, waiting for her to make a move. With a force of will, Alicia stepped away. "Ah, well, thanks for the dance. I guess I'll go try to find my friend."

Alicia walked through the crowd looking for Tina, feeling a mix of disappointment and relief. She was aroused. Her nipples were hard, and she was soaking between her legs. For the first time since she started talking to Darius, she thought of Myles at home. He'd probably be disappointed that Darius didn't pull her into his arms and dance a slow dance.

She was getting frustrated looking for Tina. Where was she? Alicia walked into a secluded, darken part of the club, far away from the lights of the dance floor, when she felt a tap on her shoulder. She turned and there was Darius, standing just inches from her. "Oh, hi—-"

Darius took her into his arms and kissed her. Alicia tried to pull away but he held her firm, his tongue pushing between her lips and exploring her mouth. His kisses were so different than Myles, who even after 10 years of marriage still kissed her softly, almost tentatively. Darius kissed her roughly, with an urgency, like kissing her was the most important thing in his life, like he wanted to own her.

Darius reached between them and cupped her breast. Even through her bra and blouse he found her hard nipple, and he roughly rubbed it with his thumb as he continued to kiss her. Alicia again tried to pull away, but Darius held her firm. With his other hand at her back, he pulled her into him. His crotch was pressed tightly against her stomach, and he felt huge.

Eventually Alicia stopped struggling. Her body couldn't resist what he was doing to her. Alicia wrapped her arms around Darius's neck and began kissing him back, swirling her tongue around his. Alicia felt terrible for returning Darius's kisses, but she told herself that Myles wanted her to do this.

Then Alicia felt Darius pull up her skirt. "No," Alicia protested.

"It's okay," Darius said. "There are rooms in the back. We can go to one."

Suddenly, Alicia knew where Tina was. And she knew she wasn't ready to take that step, not now, maybe not ever. "Please stop," Alicia said, pushing Darius away with both hands.

Darius let her go. They stood in the near darkness, inches from each other, both panting. Alicia pulled down her skirt. "I've got to go," she said.

Darius grabbed her arm. "I'll call you."

Alicia pulled her arm away and again showed him her left hand. "Married, remember?" Then Alicia hurried away, and caught a cab home.

Chapter 4

The phone rang, waking Alicia. She was still sleepy, tired from all the drinks the night before (she was probably a little hung over), and also because Myles kept her up, fucking her as she told him what happened.

"Hello?" she said into the telephone.

"You bitch!"

Alicia winced at the shoot in her ear. "Good morning Tina."

"Don't good morning me!" Tina growled. "God, I can't believe you hooked up with Darius last night. I'm so jealous! Do you know how long I've wanted that hunk?"

Alicia frowned. "Nothing happened, not really. Anyway, he started it, not me."

"Oh, that makes me feel sooooo much better. God, I can't believe it, it's just like in college, you ALWAYS get the best looking guys."

"I can't believe we're having this conversation. Are you really mad at me?"

"Yes, I'm really mad at you! And you're going to apologize by buying me lunch."

Alicia didn't want to go to lunch. She wanted to go back to bed. "Um, I'm not sure I'm up for lunch today."

"After last night, you owe me lunch! And you're going to tell me every detail of what happened with Darius!" Then Tina hung up the phone.

Alicia rolled back into bed and hugged her pillow. All she wanted to do was take two aspirin and go back to sleep. Sighing, she threw back the covers. After telling Maria, their nanny, that she was going out for lunch, she went into the bathroom.

Alicia paused to look in the mirror. Even after 10 years of marriage and 2 babies, her body was still firm. Her breasts were small, but perky, and her legs were long and shapely. Her stomach was flat, and while she had gained a little weight around the hips, she liked it because it gave her some curves that she didn't have back in college when she was stick thin.

For the first time in years, she studied herself and wondered if men still found her desirable. The thought made her feel guilty. She was married, she shouldn't be thinking about other men. But it was Myles who was encouraging her to be with other men. Last night, he was all over her as soon as she got home. He fucked her twice and seemed to stay hard the entire time as she told him what happened, the dirty dancing with Tina, and her naughtiness with Darius. She felt so guilty. But Myles had kissed away her tears and soothed her feelings, and assured her over and over again that she had done exactly what he wanted her to do. He said, in fact, he wished she had gone farther with Darius.

Earlier that morning, with the good sense that a new day brings, Alicia had worried Myles would be upset with her. But instead, Myles had awoken with a hard-on, and he fucked her again before he had to go to his office to get some things ready for a meeting he had on Monday.

She didn't know how she felt about Myles's fantasies, and this game they were playing. It was exciting, yes. But she knew this was wrong. She was no longer single. She was happily married, and happily married wives aren't supposed to act like she did last night.

But then, husbands weren't supposed to encourage their wives to be with, and even have sex with, other men. So where did that leave her? Shaking her head, she stepped into the shower.

SNEAK PEEK – FAITHFUL WIFE'S FALL FROM GRACE BOOK 1

My name's Jen. Okay, here are my stats. I'm 29, natural blonde hair that goes past my shoulders, blue eyes, about 5'4", petite with (what my husband calls) tiny tits. My best assets, I think, are my pretty face (at least I'm told I'm pretty), long legs and firm butt. I modeled a little in college and my agent (yeah, I even had an agent) said I had a future, but then I met Mike and that, as they say, was that.

Mike's my husband. He's 32. We've been together almost 10 years.

I met Mike when I was a senior in college and he was a grad student. I guess you'd call it love at first sight. We met at a mixer at my sorority and he took me to a Bruce Springsteen concert (I love the Boss!). After that we were inseparable. After graduation I moved with him to New York City. We lived together for about a year. He took me to dinner at *Per Se* and proposed. I said *yes* of course. A year later we were married.

That was 5 years ago. We're happy, although not like newlyweds anymore. We're settled in. It's comfortable, secure, you know?

Before Mike, I dated Colin. He was my high school sweetheart and we dated in college too (we all went to Penn State). Towards the end we were dating more out of habit than love. Really, we were more like fuck buddies than girlfriend/boyfriend, and he cheated on me more than once. I admit though, and I'm not proud of it, that I cheated on Colin too.

In fact, technically I was cheating on Colin the first time Mike and I had sex, although that's another story. Mike and Colin hate each other, which I guess makes sense. It doesn't matter, because I haven't seen Colin since graduation, and I doubt I'll ever seen him again in my life.

So anyways, there you go. I've had 2 serious relationships in my life, Mike and Colin, and I married Mike.

You probably want to know about our sex life. Of course, when we first met, we couldn't keep our hands off each other. And back then I was kinda a freak. I loved sex. Probably because Colin and I did it so much. I was used to getting it all the time. And Colin was an awesome lover. A shithead, but awesome in bed. I've never told Mike that, of course. He gets really jealous, especially when it comes to Colin.

But anyways, I'm just trying to explain why I was such a sex freak when Mike and I started dating. Not that Mike minded. He couldn't get enough of me. He's really into the blonde hair, long legs thing. And he doesn't care I'm practically flat chested. Unlike Colin, who never stopped talking about "pumping up my tits" (his words, not mine) as soon as he got his first NFL paycheck (Colin played football for Penn State, and even played in the NFL for a couple years until he hurt his knee). But Mike's never said that, not even once. That's one reason I love him. Because he loves me for me, just the way I am.

But back to our sex life. Okay, I admit, it's not as crazy as before. Like I said, we're settled in. Mike works really hard, and he has to travel a lot. He works on Wall Street and he's up for partnership next year, so he's doing everything he can to make his mark.

I guess I'd like sex more often (although I'm not nearly the sex freak as before). More than the sex, I'd like to be with Mike more. He works so much. I guess I'm a little lonely. But I know it's because he's trying to make a better life for us, not just the 2 of us, but for our future children. So don't mind me. I'm fine. I love Mike. We have a good marriage, we're really happy. Life is good.

I'm an account manager for a marketing firm. I like my job. It's creative and challenging to put together marketing strategies and campaigns for clients.

Back in high school and college, I dreamed about dancing, and New York City is perfect for that with all the shows on Broadway and off-Broadway. One problem with that though – I'm really not that good. I mean I'm awesome in clubs, and Mike always says he loves to watch me dance, but a stage in front of an audience is a whole different thing. So that's how I ended up in marketing.

Sometimes I think about modeling again for the glamour and excitement, but I'm afraid to bring it up with Mike. He's super sweet and loving, but he's really jealous, and the last time I brought it up we got into a big fight. I hate arguing. So I haven't mentioned it since then.

But it's probably for the best. Because you know what you have to wear when you're a model? High heels! Tall freaking high heels!

I hate heels. They are *SO - FREAKING - UNCOMFORTABLE*! It's ironic though, because Mike loves seeing me in heels, so you'd think he'd want me to model. But no, that's not how his head works. I don't think he wants me to draw attention to myself. You know, attention from other men.

Mike has a young friend, Joey. He's 14 years younger than Mike.

Mike met Joey when he was 8, about the same time we started dating. Joey and his parents lived in the apartment next to Mike's.

Back then, Mike kind of helped Joey grow up as his parents were working all the time. They became good friends. I got to know Joey too. I always thought he was a sweet boy.

Because of the age difference, Joey always looked up to Mike like a mentor, or even a hero. And Mike has always been protective of Joey.

That was 10 years ago. Joey's 18 now. Like I said, Mike's 32 and I'm 29.

Recently, Joey got accepted to NYU. School was beginning in September, so Joey moved in with us a few weeks before to get settled. I hadn't seen him in almost 4 years and *boy* did he grow up. Now he's taller than me, taller than Mike too. He must be over 6 feet. He's bigger across the chest too. He told me he wrestled the last 2 years of high school.

Joey's really handsome too. He was always a cute kid, but now the cupid face he had as a boy had matured into a very handsome young man's face.

His personality grew up too. He was still sweet, but not shy anymore. He was outgoing and confident. I was really amazed at how much he had changed. It was kind of funny how Joey had changed so much, but Mike was still the geeky, shy guy I met back in college.

Joey wasn't around a lot during those weeks before school started. I got the impression he was hanging around with friends and trying to hook up with girls. Since he was handsome and had a nice body (from what I could tell), I was pretty sure he was good with the girls. I realized he was a *player*. And that made me grin. That was another difference between Joey and Mike. Mike was, and still is, shy and awkward around girls. In fact, *I* practically had to ask *him* out on our first date. I don't mind though. I like the way Mike is shy and geeky. I love it actually. I think it's endearing.

About a week after Joey moved in, I got home from work. The apartment was empty. I figured Joey was out with his friends, as usual. But then I heard sounds coming out of the guest room where Joey slept.

I was curious, so I moved over to the guest room. The sounds were muffled. I opened the door.

My eyes went wide. Joey was in bed with a girl. They were both naked, he was on top, and he was fucking the girl really hard.

I immediately turned away and slammed the door shut. I sat on the sofa, feeling mortified.

Then I went into the kitchen. I poured a glass of wine and took a big gulp, trying to calm down.

I hadn't seen much before I turned away. Mostly just naked bodies moving.

But one thing I did see. I saw Joey's cock as he pushed in and out of the girl's pussy. And it looked huge! Long and thick!

Joey and the girl came out of the bedroom a few minutes later. They were both dressed (thankfully!). The girl introduced herself as Mary, a junior at NYU. She apologized and quickly left our apartment.

Joey said, "Sorry about that. I should have locked the door."

"Sorry I ... interrupted you," I sputtered. My cheeks were burning. I felt completely embarrassed.

"Yeah, that kind of sucks," Joey said with a laugh. As I suspected, my interruption had prevented them from completing. From cumming.

The craziness of the situation got to me, and I laughed. I said, "I'll try not to cock block you next time."

Joey laughed back.

Then he did something I'll never forget. Joey looked me up and down. He took a long look. It was like he was undressing me with his eyes. He looked at me like he was trying to figure out if he could use my body to finish what he'd started with Mary.

I muttered something and hurriedly went into the bedroom I shared with Mike. I was breathing hard as I sat on the edge of the bed.

When I was younger, before I started dating Mike, men looked at me like that all the time. Like I was a piece of meat. Like I was a girl they wanted to fuck.

Men paid a lot of attention to me. They flirted with me. I got hit on all the time. The way Joey had just treated me, it reminded me of how those men used to treat me.

Back then, I didn't like it. I didn't like being objectified. I didn't like being treated like the only thing I had to offer to the world was to be a sex toy for horny men.

But all of a sudden, I realized I missed it. I mean, I guess I know I'm pretty. I've always gotten a lot of male attention. And I told you how I was a model for a while.

But things are different when you're married. You're off the market, and men know you're off the market. They stop looking, or maybe you stop noticing they're looking. And then your husband doesn't pay as much attention to you as before. So, you start wondering if you're still pretty. If you're still attractive to men.

The way Joey just looked at me ... it made me feel good. It made me feel like I was still sexy and attractive.

———◉———

A few days later, I was home from work. Mike was traveling for business like he was doing a lot nowadays.

I was doing laundry. I had a pile of sheets and towels that we stored in the guest room closet. I opened the door and gawked at what I saw.

Joey was on the bed. He was naked on his back. His eyes were closed, and he was jerking off his big hard cock.

"Joey, fuck!" I cried as I dropped the towels and sheets and ran from the room.

A moment later Joey ran out with a towel around his waist. "You could knock, you know," he said to me.

"You can freaking lock the door!" I screamed at him. "I didn't even know you were home!"

Joey poured me a big glass of wine. He handed it to me and sat next to me on the sofa.

"Sorry about that," Joey said. "I guess you and Mike can't wait to get rid of me."

My heart softened. This was sweet Joey after all, and I'd watched him grow up. "It's not that Joey," I said. "I get you're young. You've got needs." With a laugh, I said "You just have to remember to lock the door."

Then Joey did something completely unexpected. He put his hand on my knee. I was wearing my skirt from work, and I'd taken off my pantyhose when I got home. So, his hand was on my bare knee.

"Joey, why is your hand on my knee?" I asked him stupidly.

Then Joey leaned over and kissed me. He kissed me!

Then he put his hand on my breast! This freaking kid was kissing me and fondling my breast!

"Joey what the fuck!" I said, jerking away from him. "I'm married! And my husband is your good friend!"

"Jen, I've always had a big crush on you," Joey said. "You're so pretty and sexy. When you just caught me jerking off? I was fantasizing about you."

"Joey stop talking like that!" I yelled. "Just stop!"

⬥

I didn't see Joey for a couple days. I assumed he was staying with friends. And Mike was still traveling for work.

Being alone gave me time to think. I thought about how Joey so clearly wanted me. Was he the only one? Did other men want me too?

That's how it used to be when I was younger. Men hit on me all the time. They bought my drinks in bars. They asked me on dates. They tried to kiss me and touch my body. They tried to get me into bed. It was constant.

Back then, I didn't like it. But now, looking back, I realize it was fun and exciting. It's thrilling to be chased. To be so desired.

I frowned and pursed my lips as I thought about my husband Mike. He used to be that way. When we first started dating, Mike couldn't get enough of me. His hands were always on me. Honestly, that first year, I almost broke up with him because he seemed too easy. Too desperate. But then I got to know him better. All the wonderful things about him, it took time to see them, they were under the surface. Mike was shy and awkward. So, it took time for me to realize how great a catch he was.

Especially since Mike was insecure about Colin. He always worried I was going to break up with him to get back together with my old boyfriend. After all, Colin was the star quarterback. Mike was unsure how to compete. It didn't help that Colin pursued me back then, during those early days of me and Mike dating. Eventually though, Mike got more secure about our relationship. But like I already said, he's still intensely jealous even today.

Those early years, Mike was all over me. I was the center of his world. Of his universe. We call each other "baby," that's our pet name for each other. Also, he started calling me "his goddess" sometimes. I loved it. If you've ever been in love, you know how wonderful it is to be so loved – and *even adored*—by the person you love.

But then Mike got busy with his job. He's working on something called the "Sapphire" project. Really though it started before that. Maybe 2 years ago. I don't feel like the center of his universe anymore. And I can't remember the last time he called me his goddess.

I don't know what it is. I still look the same as before. I haven't gained weight, I work out, I still have the same figure. I think I'm still pretty. Hopefully I'm still sexy. I see men looking at me. At work, on the subway, even in the grocery store. I see men looking at me. I don't flirt like I used to, because I know how much Mike hates that.

So, I think I'm still attractive to men. But Mike's not as hot for me anymore. It used to be, he wanted sex every day, sometimes more than once. Now, it seems like I'm the one initiating it most times.

It's not just us though. I think maybe that's how it is with all married couples. My best friend Allie, she's going through the same thing. The red-hot intensity at the beginning of the romance starts to cool off after you get married, as the years go by. There's less flowers, less sweet nothings, less sex. You kinda settle into a routine. It's comfortable, secure. I'm happy. But I guess sometimes I miss the romance. You know, the infatuation. The passion. I guess maybe I wish Mike would call me "his goddess" again. It doesn't have to be all the time. Just sometimes, the way it used to be.

I took a shower. I had a towel around me as I brushed my damp hair. My eyes were off into the distance as I thought about where my life was. I still loved Mike. I did. I really loved him. But I wasn't happy. I wanted excitement. I wanted passion. Mike gave me a lot of things – kindness, security, stability. He gave me love.

But he wasn't giving me excitement and passion. At least, not anymore. And I wasn't happy. I was content. But not happy.

At that moment, I heard a sound behind me. I turned and saw it was Joey.

I tightened the towel around me. "Have you ever heard of knocking?" I asked.

"I guess this time it was you who didn't lock the door," he joked with a grin.

Joey moved towards me. He moved behind me. He pressed against my back.

"Joey ...," I began in protest.

He kissed my bare shoulder and my breath caught.

Then he kissed up my neck. My heart began pounding in my chest.

I was holding the top of the towel with my hand, to keep it from opening.

Joey put his hand over mine. He reached around my hand and took hold of the towel.

"Joey ...," I said again. Before I could say anything else, he pulled the towel off me. The towel fell to the floor.

Suddenly, I was completely naked with this 18-year-old boy standing behind me.

Joey kissed my neck again. He kissed just below my ear, one of my major erogenous spots, and my eyes fluttered.

Joey reached to my front with both hands, and he cupped my naked breasts.

"Joey ...," I said once more. This time he's name came out like a moan.

I turned my head to look at him, to tell him to stop. I think I was going to tell him to stop. But it didn't matter. Before I could say anything, he was kissing me. He kissed me and fondled my breasts. I moaned into his mouth as he rubbed my nipples with his thumbs.

Then we walked / stumbled on to the bed. Joey got on top of me. His lips never left mine. And by this time, I was kissing him back.

Joey reached between us and urgently pulled down his pants. I felt his hard, large cock pressing against my thigh.

Joey used his knees to open my legs. It was clear he'd done this before, with other girls. Yes, no doubt, he was a player.

He took hold of his cock and guided it to my pussy. Then he pushed in.

Just like that, another man's cock was inside me. Just like that, I was cheating on Mike for the first time. Just like that, I was an unfaithful wife.

And to make it all worse, Joey was only 18. I was 11 years older than him. And he was good friends with my husband.

I grimaced as Joey pushed his cock into me. I wasn't used to his size – he was big!—and it hurt at first. But soon the pain felt good. Joey's cock reminded me of Colin's, my boyfriend before Mike. Colin was a horrible boyfriend and he treated me like shit, but he always fucked me good.

That's what Joey was doing now. He was fucking me good.

When I came, my orgasm was so intense I saw stars. And I think I screamed.

Moments later, Joey grunted violently as his own orgasm hit. He jack-rabbited hard and fast into my pussy as he ejaculated streams of his cum into me.

After, we looked at each other, panting into each other's face as we recovered from our orgasms.

"Joey, you need to get off me," I managed to say between pants, pushing up on his chest with my hands.

He nodded. He pulled his softening cock from my pussy. With a last look at me, he left my bedroom and closed the door.

I didn't move for a long time. I felt horrible of course. I'd just cheated on Mike. I felt so guilty.

But then a slight grin crept onto my face. Holy fuck. Joey had just fucked my brains out. My body was still tingling. He was only 18 – how the heck did he learn to fuck like that? Of course, I thought with a giggle, he did have the equipment for it.

These thoughts made me feel even more guilty. I wanted to call my best friend Allie to tell her what happened. She would understand because I knew she'd slipped up in her marriage too. More than once, actually. But Joey was so young. I wasn't sure even Allie would have sex with an 18-year-old.

I knew I had to talk to Joey. I had to get him to promise to never tell Mike. To never tell anyone.

People made mistakes sometimes. And this was definitely a mistake.

But there was no reason for Mike to ever know. I was 100% faithful before today, and I'd be 100% faithful from now on. I slipped up, and it would be my one and only slip up. Mike would never find out. And I would never cheat on him again.

When I woke up the next morning, Joey wasn't home. I figured he was staying with friends again.

It was kind of a relief. I needed to talk to him, but I didn't *want* to talk to him. So, I wasn't disappointed when I didn't see or hear from him. At least he wasn't trying to get into my pants again. He said he'd harbored a crush on me for years. Maybe he didn't anymore after getting me to bed. And I was completely okay with that.

I needed to talk to Joey, but I figured there was no rush. I figured he wasn't stupid enough to say anything to Mike.

Don't miss out!

Visit the website below and you can sign up to receive emails whenever Pete Andrews publishes a new book. There's no charge and no obligation.

https://books2read.com/r/B-A-KWSAB-KYUOC

BOOKS 2 READ

Connecting independent readers to independent writers.